Lord Lyttelton – Dialogues Of The Dead

Sir George Lyttelton, 1st Baron Lyttelton PC was born on January 17th, 1709, the son of Sir Thomas Lyttelton, 4th Baronet, and his wife Christian, daughter of Sir Richard Temple, 3rd Baronet.

George was educated at Eton and Christ Church, Oxford.

In the 1730's he was a great friend and supporter to the extraordinary poet, Alexander Pope.

In 1735 he was elected to be the Member of Parliament for Okehampton, a seat that he served until 1756. Interestingly in 1741 he was also elected for Old Sarum, but chose to continue to sit for Okehampton.

In politics he was a Whig, in opposition, and therefore opposed to Robert Walpole.

He served as secretary to Frederick, Prince of Wales, from 1737, and as a Commissioner of the Treasury in 1744. With the fall of Walpole Lyttelton became Chancellor of the Exchequer in 1755.

The following year he was raised to the peerage as Lord Lyttelton, Baron of Frankley in the County of Worcester.

In these years he also supported and was friends with the author Henry Fielding, who dedicated his great novel 'Tom Jones' to him and to the poet James Thomson who addressed him throughout his poem 'The Seasons'. Lyttelton thereafter arranged a pension for Thomson.

In 1760 he wrote Dialogues of the Dead with Elizabeth Montagu, leader of the bluestockings. It is the work for which his name is remembered to this day. He also wrote 'The History of the Life of Henry the Second (1767–1771).

Lyttelton spent many years and a fortune developing Hagley Hall and its park which contains many follies. The hall itself, which is in north Worcestershire, was designed by Sanderson Miller and is the last of the great Palladian houses to be built in England.

George Lyttelton died on August 24th, 1773, and was buried in Christ Church Cathedral.

Index Of Contents

INTRODUCTION.

George, Lord Lyttelton, was born in 1709, at Hagley, in Worcestershire. He was educated at Eton and at Christchurch, Oxford, entered Parliament, became a Lord of the Treasury and Chancellor of the Exchequer. In 1757 he withdrew from politics, was raised to the peerage, and spent the last eighteen years of his life in lettered ease. In 1760 Lord Lyttelton first published these "Dialogues of the Dead," which were revised for a fourth edition in 1765, and in 1767 he published in four volumes a "History of the Life of King Henry the Second and of the Age in which he Lived," a work upon which he had been busy for thirty years. He began it not long after he had published, at the age of twenty-six, his "Letters from a Persian in England to his Friend at Ispahan." If we go farther back we find George Lyttelton, aged twenty-three, beginning his life in literature as a poet, with four eclogues on "The Progress of Love."

To the last Lord Lyttelton was poet enough to feel true fellowship with poets of his day. He loved good literature, and his own works show that he knew it. He counted Henry Fielding among his friends; he was a friend and helper to James Thomson, the author of "The Seasons;" and when acting as secretary to the king's son, Frederick, Prince of Wales (who held a little court of his own, in which there was much said about liberty), his friendship brought Thomson and Mallet together in work on a masque for the Prince and Princess, which included the song of "Rule Britannia."

Before Lord Lyttelton followed their example, "Dialogues of the Dead" had been written by Lucian, and by Fenelon, and by Fontenelle; and in our time they have been written by Walter Savage Landor. This half-dramatic plan of presenting a man's own thoughts upon the life of man and characters of men, and on the issues of men's characters in shaping life, is a way of essay writing pleasant alike to the writer and the reader. Lord Lyttelton was at his best in it. The form of writing obliged him to work with a lighter touch than he used when he sought to maintain the dignity of history by the style of his "History of Henry II." His calm liberality of mind enters into the discussion of many topics. His truths are old, but there are no real truths of human life and conduct, worth anything at all, that are of yesterday. Human love itself is called "the old, old story;" but do we therefore cease from loving, or from finding such ways as we can of saying that we love. Dr. Johnson was not at his wisest when he found fault with Lord Lyttelton because, in his "Dialogues of the Dead," "that man sat down to write a book, to tell the world what the world had all his life been telling him." This was exactly what he wished to do. In the Preface to his revised edition Lord Lyttelton said, "Sometimes a new dress may render an old truth more pleasing to those whom the mere love of novelty betrays into error, as it frequently does not only the wits, but the sages of these days. Indeed, one of the best services that could now be done to mankind by any good writer would be the bringing them back to common sense, from which the desire of shining by extraordinary notions has seduced great numbers, to the no small detriment of morality and of all real knowledge."

At any rate, we now find it worth while to know what the world had been telling all his life to an enlightened, highly-educated man, who was an active politician in the days of Walpole and of the elder Pitt, who was a friend of Pope's and of the best writers of the day, and who in his occasional verse added at least one line to the household words of English literature when in his warm-hearted Prologue to Thomson's play of Coriolanus, produced after its writer's death, he said of that poet what we may say of Lord Lyttelton himself, that he gave to the world

"Not one immoral, one corrupted thought,   One line which, dying, he could wish to blot."

H. M.

DIALOGUE I. LORD FALKLAND - MR. HAMPDEN.

Lord Falkland. Are not you surprised to see me in Elysium, Mr. Hampden?

Mr. Hampden. I was going to put the same question to your lordship, for doubtless you thought me a rebel.

Lord Falkland. And certainly you thought me an apostate from the Commonwealth, and a supporter of tyranny.

Mr. Hampden. I own I did, and I don't wonder at the severity of your thoughts about me. The heat of the times deprived us both of our natural candour. Yet I will confess to you here, that, before I died, I began to see in our party enough to justify your apprehensions that the civil war, which we had entered into from generous motives, from a laudable desire to preserve our free constitution, would end very unhappily, and perhaps, in the issue, destroy that constitution, even by the arms of those who pretended to be most zealous for it.

Lord Falkland. And I will as frankly own to you that I saw, in the court and camp of the king, so much to alarm me for the liberty of my country, if our arms were successful, that I dreaded a victory little less than I did a defeat, and had nothing in my mouth but the word peace, which I constantly repeated with passionate fondness, in every council at which I was called to assist.

Mr. Hampden. I wished for peace too, as ardently as your lordship, but I saw no hopes of it. The insincerity of the king and the influence of the queen made it impossible to trust to his promises and declarations. Nay, what reliance could we reasonably have upon laws designed to limit and restrain the power of the Crown, after he had violated the Bill of Rights, obtained with such difficulty, and containing so clear an assertion of the privileges which had been in dispute? If his conscience would allow him to break an Act of Parliament, made to determine the bounds of the royal prerogative, because he thought that the royal prerogative could have no bounds, what legal ties could bind a conscience so prejudiced? or what effectual security could his people obtain against the obstinate malignity of such an opinion, but entirely taking from him the power of the sword, and enabling themselves to defend the laws he had passed?

Lord Falkland. There is evidently too much truth in what you have said. But by taking from the king the power of the sword, you in reality took all power. It was converting the government into a democracy; and if he had submitted to it, he would only have preserved the name of a king. The sceptre would have been held by those who had the sword; or we must have lived in a state of perpetual anarchy, without any force or balance in the government; a state which could not have lasted long, but would have ended in a republic or in absolute dominion.

Mr. Hampden. Your reasoning seems unanswerable. But what could we do? Let Dr. Laud and those other court divines, who directed the king's conscience, and fixed in it such principles as made him unfit to govern a limited monarchy, though with many good qualities, and some great ones, let them, I say, answer for all the mischiefs they brought upon him and the nation.

Lord Falkland. They were indeed much to blame; but those principles had gained ground before their times, and seemed the principles of our Church, in opposition to the Jesuits, who had certainly gone too far in the other extreme.

Mr. Hampden. It is a disgrace to our Church to have taken up such opinions; and I will venture to prophesy that our clergy in future times must renounce them, or they will be turned against them by those who mean their destruction. Suppose a Popish king on the throne, will the clergy adhere to passive obedience and non-resistance? If they do, they deliver up their religion to Rome; if they do not, their practice will confute their own doctrines.

Lord Falkland. Nature, sir, will in the end be sure to set right whatever opinion contradicts her great laws, let who will be the teacher. But, indeed, the more I reflect on those miserable times in which we both lived, the more I esteem it a favour of Providence to us that we were cut off so soon. The most grievous misfortune that can befall a virtuous man is to be in such a state that he can hardly so act as to approve his own conduct. In such a state we both were. We could not easily make a step, either forward or backward, without great hazard of guilt, or at least of dishonour. We were unhappily entangled in connections with men who did not mean so well as ourselves, or did not judge so rightly. If we endeavoured to stop them, they thought us false to the cause; if we went on with them, we ran directly upon rocks, which we saw, but could not avoid. Nor could we take shelter in a philosophical retreat from business. Inaction would in us have been cowardice and desertion. To complete the public calamities, a religious fury, on both sides, mingled itself with the rage of our civil dissensions, more frantic than that, more implacable, more averse to all healing measures. The most intemperate counsels were thought the most pious, and a regard to the laws, if they opposed the suggestions of these fiery zealots, was accounted irreligion. This added new difficulties to what was before but too difficult in itself, the settling of a nation which no longer could put any confidence in its sovereign, nor lay more restraints on the royal authority without destroying the balance of the whole constitution. In those circumstances, the balls that pierced our hearts were directed thither by the hands of our guardian angels, to deliver us from horrors we could not support, and perhaps from a guilt our souls abhorred.

Mr. Hampden. Indeed, things were brought to so deplorable a state, that if either of us had seen his party triumphant, he must have lamented that triumph as the ruin of his country. Were I to return into life, the experience I have had would make me very cautious how I kindled the sparks of civil war in England; for I have seen that, when once that devouring fire is lighted, it is not in the power of the head of a party to say to the conflagration, "Thus far shalt thou go, and here shall thy violence stop."

Lord Falkland. The conversation we have had, as well as the reflections of my own mind on past events, would, if I were condemned to my body again, teach me great moderation in my judgments of persons who might happen to differ from me in difficult scenes of public action; they would entirely cure me of the spirit of party, and make me think that as in the Church, so also in the State, no evil is more to be feared than a rancorous and enthusiastical zeal.

DIALOGUE II. LOUIS LE GRAND - PETER THE GREAT.

Louis. Who, sir, could have thought, when you were learning the trade of a shipwright in the dockyards of England and Holland, that you would ever acquire, as I had done, the surname of "Great."

Peter. Which of us best deserved that title posterity will decide. But my greatness appeared sufficiently in that very act which seemed to you a debasement.

Louis. The dignity of a king does not stoop to such mean employments. For my own part, I was careful never to appear to the eyes of my subjects or foreigners but in all the splendour and majesty of royal power.

Peter. Had I remained on the throne of Russia, as my ancestors did, environed with all the pomp of barbarous greatness, I should have been idolised by my people, as much, at least, as you ever were by the French. My despotism was more absolute, their servitude was more humble. But then I could not have reformed their evil customs; have taught them arts, civility, navigation, and war; have exalted them from brutes in human shapes into men. In this was seen the extraordinary force of my genius beyond any comparison with all other kings, that I thought it no degradation or diminution of my greatness to descend from my throne, and go and work in the dockyards of a foreign republic; to serve as a private sailor in my own fleets, and as a common soldier in my own army, till I had raised myself by my merit in all the several steps and degrees of promotion up to the highest command, and had thus induced my nobility to submit to a regular subordination in the sea and land service by a lesson hard to their pride, and which they would not have learnt from any other master or by any other method of instruction.

Louis. I am forced to acknowledge that it was a great act. When I thought it a mean one, my judgment was perverted by the prejudices arising from my own education and the ridicule thrown upon it by some of my courtiers, whose minds were too narrow to be able to comprehend the greatness of yours in that situation.

Peter. It was an act of more heroism than any ever done by Alexander or Caesar. Nor would I consent to exchange my glory with theirs. They both did great things; but they were at the head of great nations, far superior in valour and military skill to those with whom they contended. I was the king of an ignorant, undisciplined, barbarous people. My enemies were at first so superior to my subjects that ten thousand of them could beat a hundred thousand Russians. They had formidable navies; I had not a ship. The King of Sweden was a prince of the most intrepid courage, assisted by generals of consummate knowledge in war, and served by soldiers so disciplined that they were become the admiration and terror of Europe. Yet I vanquished these soldiers; I drove that prince to take refuge in Turkey; I won battles at sea as well as land; I new- created my people; I gave them arts, science, policy; I enabled them to keep all the powers of the North in awe and dependence, to give kings to Poland, to check and intimidate the Ottoman emperors, to mix with great weight in the affairs of all Europe. What other man has ever done such wonders as these? Read all the records of ancient and modern times, and find, if you can, one fit to be put in comparison with me!

Louis. Your glory would indeed have been supreme and unequalled if, in civilising your subjects, you had reformed the brutality of your own manners and the barbarous vices of your nature. But, alas! the legislator and reformer of the Muscovites was drunken and cruel.

Peter. My drunkenness I confess; nor will I plead, to excuse it, the example of Alexander. It inflamed the tempers of both, which were by nature too fiery, into furious passions of anger, and produced actions of which our reason, when sober, was ashamed. But the cruelty you upbraid me with may in some degree be excused, as necessary to the work I had to perform. Fear of punishment was in the hearts of my barbarous subjects the only principle of obedience. To make them respect the royal authority I was obliged to arm it with all the terrors of rage. You had a more pliant people to govern, a people whose minds could be ruled, like a fine-managed horse, with an easy and gentle rein. The fear of shame did more with them than the fear of the knout could do with the Russians. The humanity of your character and the ferocity of mine were equally suitable to the nations over which we reigned. But what excuse can you find for the cruel violence you employed against your Protestant subjects? They desired nothing but to live under the protection of laws you yourself had confirmed; and they repaid that protection by the most hearty zeal for your service. Yet these did you force, by the most inhuman severities, either to quit the religion in which they were bred, and which their consciences still retained, or to leave their native land, and endure all the woes of a perpetual exile. If the rules of policy could not hinder you from thus depopulating your kingdom, and transferring to foreign countries its manufactures and commerce, I am surprised that your heart itself did not stop you. It makes one shudder to think that such orders should be sent from the most polished court in Europe, as the most savage Tartars could hardly have executed without remorse and compassion.

Louis. It was not my heart, but my religion, that dictated these severities. My confessor told me they alone would atone for all my sins.

Peter. Had I believed in my patriarch as you believed in your priest, I should not have been the great monarch that I was. But I mean not to detract from the merit of a prince whose memory is dear to his subjects. They are proud of having obeyed you, which is certainly the highest praise to a king. My people also date their glory from the era of my reign. But there is this capital distinction between us. The pomp and pageantry of state were necessary to your greatness; I was great in myself, great in the energy and powers of my mind, great in the superiority and sovereignty of my soul over all other men.

DIALOGUE III. PLATO - FENELON.

Plato. Welcome to Elysium, O thou, the most pure, the most gentle, the most refined disciple of philosophy that the world in modern times has produced! Sage Fenelon, welcome! I need not name myself to you. Our souls by sympathy must know one another.

Fenelon. I know you to be Plato, the most amiable of all the disciples of Socrates, and the philosopher of all antiquity whom I most desired to resemble.

Plato. Homer and Orpheus are impatient to see you in that region of these happy fields which their shades inhabit. They both acknowledge you to be a great poet, though you have written no verses. And they are now busy in composing for you unfading wreaths of all the finest and sweetest Elysian flowers. But I will lead you from them to the sacred grove of philosophy, on the highest hill of Elysium, where the air is most pure and most serene. I will conduct you to the fountain of wisdom, in which you will see, as in your own writings, the fair image of virtue perpetually reflected. It will raise in you more love than was felt by Narcissus, when he contemplated the beauty of his own face in the unruffled spring. But you shall not pine, as he did, for a shadow. The goddess herself will affectionately meet your embraces and mingle with your soul.

Fenelon. I find you retain the allegorical and poetical style, of which you were so fond in many of your writings. Mine also run sometimes into poetry, particularly in my "Telemachus," which I meant to make a kind of epic composition. But I dare not rank myself among the great poets, nor pretend to any equality in oratory with you, the most eloquent of philosophers, on whose lips the Attic bees distilled all their honey.

Plato. The French language is not so harmonious as the Greek, yet you have given a sweetness to it which equally charms the ear and heart. When one reads your compositions, one thinks that one hears Apollo's lyre, strung by the hands of the Graces, and tuned by the Muses. The idea of a perfect king, which you have exhibited in your "Telemachus," far excels, in my own judgment, my imaginary "Republic." Your "Dialogues" breathe the pure spirit of virtue, of unaffected good sense, of just criticism, of fine taste. They are in general as superior to your countryman Fontenelle's as reason is to false wit, or truth to affectation. The greatest fault of them, I think, is, that some are too short.

Fenelon. It has been objected to them and I am sensible of it Myself, that most of them are too full of commonplace morals. But I wrote them for the instruction of a young prince, and one cannot too forcibly imprint on the minds of those who are born to empire the most simple truths; because, as they grow up, the flattery of a court will try to disguise and conceal from them those truths, and to eradicate from their hearts the love of their duty, if it has not taken there a very deep root.

Plato. It is, indeed, the peculiar misfortune of princes, that they are often instructed with great care in the refinements of policy, and not taught the first principles of moral obligations, or taught so superficially that the virtuous man is soon lost in the corrupt politician. But the lessons of virtue you gave your royal pupil are so graced by the charms of your eloquence that the oldest and wisest men may attend to them with pleasure. All your writings are embellished with a sublime and agreeable imagination, which gives elegance to simplicity, and dignity to the most vulgar and obvious truths. I have heard, indeed, that your countrymen are less sensible of the beauty of your genius and style than any of their neighbours. What has so much depraved their taste?

Fenelon. That which depraved the taste of the Romans after the ago of Augustus, an immoderate love of wit, of paradox, of refinement. The works of their writers, like the faces of their women, must be painted and adorned with artificial embellishments to attract their regards. And thus the natural beauty of both is lost. But it is no wonder if few of them esteem my "Telemachus," as the maxims I have principally inculcated there are thought by many inconsistent with the grandeur of their monarchy, and with the splendour of a refined and opulent nation. They seem generally to be falling into opinions that the chief end of society is to procure the pleasures of luxury; that a nice and elegant taste of voluptuous enjoyments is the perfection of merit; and that a king, who is gallant, magnificent, liberal, who builds a fine palace, who furnishes it well with good statues and pictures, who encourages the fine arts, and makes them subservient to every modish vice, who has a restless ambition, a perfidious policy, and a spirit of conquest, is better for them than a Numa or a Marcus Aurelius. Whereas to check the excesses of luxury, those excesses, I mean, which enfeeble the spirit of a nation, to ease the people, as much as is possible, of the burden of taxes; to give them the blessings of peace and tranquillity, when they can he obtained without injury or dishonour; to make them frugal, and hardy, and masculine in the temper of their bodies and minds, that they may be the fitter for war whenever it does come upon them; but, above all, to watch diligently over their morals, and discourage whatever may defile or corrupt them, is the great business of government, and ought to be in all circumstances the principal object of a wise legislature. Unquestionably that is the happiest country which has most virtue in it; and to the eye of sober reason the poorest Swiss canton is a much nobler state than the kingdom of France, if it has more liberty, better morals, a more settled tranquillity, more moderation in prosperity, and more firmness in danger.

Plato. Your notions are just, and if your country rejects them she will not long hold the rank of the first nation in Europe. Her declension is begun, her ruin approaches; for, omitting all other arguments, can a state be well served when the raising of an opulent fortune in its service, and making a splendid use of that fortune, is a distinction more envied than any which arises from integrity in office or public spirit in government? Can that spirit, which is the parent of national greatness, continue vigorous and diffusive where the desire of wealth, for the sake of a luxury which wealth alone can support, and an ambition aspiring, not to glory, but to profit, are the predominant passions? If it exists in a king or a minister of state, how will either of them find among a people so disposed the necessary instruments to execute his great designs; or, rather, what obstruction will he not find from the continual opposition of private interest to public? But if, on the contrary, a court inclines to tyranny, what a facility will be given by these dispositions to that evil purpose? How will men with minds relaxed by the enervating ease and softness of luxury have vigour to oppose it? Will not most of them lean to servitude, as their natural state, as that in which the extravagant and insatiable cravings of their artificial wants may best be gratified at the charge of a bountiful master or by the spoils of an enslaved and ruined people? When all sense of public virtue is thus destroyed, will not fraud, corruption, and avarice, or the opposite workings of court factions to bring disgrace on each other, ruin armies and fleets without the help of an enemy, and give up the independence of the nation to foreigners, after having betrayed its liberties to a king? All these mischiefs you saw attendant on that luxury, which some modern philosophers account (as I am informed) the highest good to a state! Time will show that their doctrines are pernicious to society, pernicious to government; and that yours, tempered and moderated so as to render them more practicable in the present circumstances of your country, are wise, salutary, and deserving of the general thanks of mankind. But lest you should think, from the praise I have given you, that flattery can find a place in Elysium, allow me to lament, with the tender sorrow of a friend, that a man so superior to all other follies could give into the reveries of a Madame Guyon, a distracted enthusiast. How strange was it to see the two great lights of France, you and the Bishop of Meaux, engaged in a controversy whether a madwoman was a heretic or a saint!

Fenelon. I confess my own weakness, and the ridiculousness of the dispute; but did not your warm imagination carry you also into some reveries about divine love, in which you talked unintelligibly, even to yourself?

Plato. I felt something more than I was able to express.

Fenelon. I had my feelings too, as fine and as lively as yours; but we should both have done better to have avoided those subjects in which sentiment took the place of reason.

DIALOGUE IV. MR. ADDISON - DR. SWIFT.

Dr. Swift. Surely, Addison, Fortune was exceedingly inclined to play the fool (a humour her ladyship, as well as most other ladies of very great quality, is frequently in) when she made you a minister of state and me a divine!

Addison. I must confess we were both of us out of our elements; but you don't mean to insinuate that all would have been right if our destinies had been reversed?

Swift. Yes, I do. You would have made an excellent bishop, and I should have governed Great Britain, as I did Ireland, with an absolute sway, while I talked of nothing but liberty, property, and so forth.

Addison. You governed the mob of Ireland; but I never understood that you governed the kingdom. A nation and a mob are very different things.

Swift. Ay, so you fellows that have no genius for politics may suppose; but there are times when, by seasonably putting himself at the head of the mob, an able man may get to the head of the nation. Nay, there are times when the nation itself is a mob, and ought to be treated as such by a skilful observer.

Addison. I don't deny the truth of your proposition; but is there no danger that, from the natural vicissitudes of human affairs, the favourite of the mob should be mobbed in his turn?

Swift. Sometimes there may be, but I risked it, and it answered my purpose. Ask the lord-lieutenants, who were forced to pay court to me instead of my courting them, whether they did not feel my superiority. And if I could make myself so considerable when I was only a dirty Dean of St. Patrick's, without a seat in either House of Parliament, what should I have done if Fortune had placed me in England, unencumbered with a gown, and in a situation that would have enabled me to make myself heard in the House of Lords or of Commons?

Addison. You would undoubtedly have done very marvellous acts! Perhaps you might then have been as zealous a Whig as my Lord Wharton himself; or, if the Whigs had unhappily offended the statesman as they did the doctor, who knows whether you might not have brought in the Pretender? Pray let me ask you one question between you and me: If your great talents had raised you to the office of first minister under that prince, would you have tolerated the Protestant religion or not?

Swift. Ha! Mr. Secretary, are you witty upon me? Do you think, because Sunderland took a fancy to make you a great man in the state, that he, or his master, could make you as great in wit as Nature made me? No, no; wit is like grace, it must be given from above. You can no more get that from the king than my lords the bishops can the other. And, though I will own you had some, yet believe me, my good friend, it was no match for mine. I think you have not vanity enough in your nature to pretend to a competition in that point with me.

Addison. I have been told by my friends that I was rather too modest, so I will not determine this dispute for myself, but refer it to Mercury, the god of wit, who fortunately happens to be coming this way with a soul he has brought to the Shades.

Hail, divine Hermes! A question of precedence in the class of wit and humour, over which you preside, having arisen between me and my countryman, Dr. Swift, we beg leave

Mercury. Dr. Swift, I rejoice to see you. How does my old lad? How does honest Lemuel Gulliver? Have you been in Lilliput lately, or in the Flying Island, or with your good nurse Glumdalclitch? Pray when did you eat a crust with Lord Peter? Is Jack as mad still as ever? I hear that since you published the history of his case the poor fellow, by more gentle usage, is almost got well. If he had but more food he would be as much in his senses as Brother Martin himself; but Martin, they tell me, has lately spawned a strange brood of Methodists, Moravians, Hutchinsonians, who are madder than ever Jack was in his worst days. It is a great pity you are not alive again to make a new edition of your "Tale of the Tub" for the use of these fellows. Mr. Addison, I beg your pardon; I should have spoken to you sooner, but I was so struck with the sight of my old friend the doctor, that I forgot for a time the respects due to you.

Swift. Addison, I think our dispute is decided before the judge has heard the cause.

Addison. I own it is in your favour, but

Mercury. Don't be discouraged, friend Addison. Apollo perhaps would have given a different judgment. I am a wit, and a rogue, and a foe to all dignity. Swift and I naturally like one another. He worships me more than Jupiter, and I honour him more than Homer; but yet, I assure you, I have a great value for you. Sir Roger de Coverley, Will Honeycomb, Will Wimble, the Country Gentleman in the Freeholder, and twenty more characters, drawn with the finest strokes of unaffected wit and humour in your admirable writings, have obtained for you a high place in the class of my authors, though not quite so high a one as the Dean of St. Patrick's. Perhaps you might have got before him if the decency of your nature and the cautiousness of your judgment would have given you leave. But, allowing that in the force and spirit of his wit he has really the advantage, how much does he yield to you in all the elegant graces, in the fine touches of delicate sentiment, in developing the secret springs of the soul, in showing the mild lights and shades of a character, in distinctly marking each line, and every soft gradation of tints, which would escape the common eye? Who ever painted like you the beautiful parts of human nature, and brought them out from under the shade even of the greatest simplicity, or the most ridiculous weaknesses; so that we are forced to admire and feel that we venerate, even while we are laughing? Swift was able to do nothing that approaches to this. He could draw an ill face, or caricature a good one, with a masterly hand; but there was all his power, and, if I am to speak as a god, a worthless power it is. Yours is divine. It tends to exalt human nature.

Swift. Pray, good Mercury (if I may have liberty to say a word for myself) do you think that my talent was not highly beneficial to correct human nature? Is whipping of no use to mend naughty boys?

Mercury. Men are generally not so patient of whipping as boys, and a rough satirist is seldom known to mend them. Satire, like antimony, if it be used as a medicine, must be rendered less corrosive. Yours is often rank poison. But I will allow that you have done some good in your way, though not half so much as Addison did in his.

Addison. Mercury, I am satisfied. It matters little what rank you assign me as a wit, if you give me the precedence as a friend and benefactor to mankind.

Mercury. I pass sentence on the writers, not the men, and my decree is this: When any hero is brought hither who wants to be humbled, let the talk of lowering his arrogance be assigned to Swift.

The same good office may be done to a philosopher vain of his wisdom and virtue, or to a bigot puffed up with spiritual pride. The doctor's discipline will soon convince the first, that with all his boasted morality, he is but a Yahoo; and the latter, that to be holy he must necessarily be humble. I would also have him apply his anticosmetic wash to the painted face of female vanity, and his rod, which draws blood at every stroke, to the hard back of insolent folly or petulant wit. But Addison should be employed to comfort those whose delicate minds are dejected with too painful a sense of some infirmities in their nature. To them he should hold his fair and charitable mirror, which would bring to their sight their hidden excellences, and put them in a temper fit for Elysium. Adieu. Continue to esteem and love each other, as you did in the other world, though you were of opposite parties, and, what is still more wonderful, rival wits. This alone is sufficient to entitle you both to Elysium.

DIALOGUE V. ULYSSES - CIRCE - IN CIRCE'S ISLAND.

Circe. You will go then, Ulysses, but tell me, without reserve, what carries you from me?

Ulysses. Pardon, goddess, the weakness of human nature. My heart will sigh for my country. It is an attachment which all my admiration of you cannot entirely overcome.

Circe. This is not all. I perceive you are afraid to declare your whole mind. But what, Ulysses, do you fear? My terrors are gone. The proudest goddess on earth, when she has favoured a mortal as I have favoured you, has laid her divinity and power at his feet.

Ulysses. It may be so while there still remains in her heart the tenderness of love, or in her mind the fear of shame. But you, Circe, are above those vulgar sensations.

Circe. I understand your caution; it belongs to your character, and therefore, to remove all diffidence from you, I swear by Styx I will do no manner of harm, either to you or your friends, for anything which you say, however offensive it may be to my love or my pride, but will send you away from my island with all marks of my friendship. Tell me now, truly, what pleasures you hope to enjoy in the barren rock of Ithaca, which can compensate for those you leave in this paradise, exempt from all cares and overflowing with all delights?

Ulysses. The pleasures of virtue; the supreme happiness of doing good. Here I do nothing. My mind is in a palsy; all its faculties are benumbed. I long to return into action, that I may worthily employ those talents which I have cultivated from the earliest days of my youth. Toils and cares fright not me; they are the exercise of my soul; they keep it in health and in vigour. Give me again the fields of Troy, rather than these vacant groves. There I could reap the bright harvest of glory; here I am hid like a coward from the eyes of mankind, and begin to appear comtemptible in my own. The image of my former self haunts and seems to upbraid me wheresoever I go. I meet it under the gloom of every shade; it even intrudes itself into your presence and chides me from your arms. O goddess, unless you have power to lay that spirit, unless you can make me forget myself, I cannot be happy here, I shall every day be more wretched.

Circe. May not a wise and good man, who has spent all his youth in active life and honourable danger, when he begins to decline, be permitted to retire and enjoy the rest of his days in quiet and pleasure?

Ulysses. No retreat can be honourable to a wise and good man but in company with the muses. Here I am deprived of that sacred society. The muses will not inhabit the abodes of voluptuousness and sensual pleasure. How can I study or think while such a number of beasts and the worst beasts are men turned into beasts are howling or roaring or grunting all about me?

Circe. There may be something in this, but this I know is not all. You suppress the strongest reason that draws you to Ithaca. There is another image besides that of your former self, which appears to you in this island, which follows you in your walks, which more particularly interposes itself between you and me, and chides you from my arms. It is Penelope, Ulysses, I know it is. Don't pretend to deny it. You sigh for Penelope in my bosom itself. And yet she is not an immortal. She is not, as I am, endowed by Nature with the gift of unfading youth. Several years have passed since hers has been faded. I might say, without vanity, that in her best days she was never so handsome as I. But what is she now?

Ulysses. You have told me yourself, in a former conversation, when I inquired of you about her, that she is faithful to my bed, and as fond of me now, after twenty years' absence, as at the time when I left her to go to Troy. I left her in the bloom of youth and beauty. How much must her constancy have been tried since that time! How meritorious is her fidelity! Shall I reward her with falsehood? Shall I forget my Penelope, who can't forget me, who has no pleasure so dear to her as my remembrance?

Circe. Her love is preserved by the continual hope of your speedy return. Take that hope from her. Let your companions return, and let her know that you have fixed your abode with me, that you have fixed it for ever. Let her know that she is free to dispose as she pleases of her heart and her hand. Send my picture to her, bid her compare it with her own face. If all this does not cure her of the remains of her passion, if you don't hear of her marrying Eurymachus in a twelvemonth, I understand nothing of womankind.

Ulysses. O cruel goddess! why will you force me to tell you truths I desire to conceal? If by such unmerited, such barbarous usage I could lose her heart it would break mine. How should I be able to endure the torment of thinking that I had wronged such a wife? What could make me amends for her being no longer mine, for her being another's? Don't frown, Circe, I must own, since you will have me speak, I must own you could not. With all your pride of immortal beauty, with all your magical charms to assist those of Nature, you are not so powerful a charmer as she. You feel desire, and you give it, but you have never felt love, nor can you inspire it. How can I love one who would have degraded me into a beast? Penelope raised me into a hero. Her love ennobled, invigorated, exalted my mind. She bid me go to the siege of Troy, though the parting with me was worse than death to herself. She bid me expose myself there to all the perils of war among the foremost heroes of Greece, though her poor heart sunk and trembled at every thought of those perils, and would have given all its own blood to save a drop of mine. Then there was such a conformity in all our inclinations! When Minerva was teaching me the lessons of wisdom she delighted to be present. She heard, she retained, she gave them back to me softened and sweetened with the peculiar graces of her own mind. When we unbent our thoughts with the charms of poetry, when we read together the poems of Orpheus, Musaeus, and Linus, with what taste did she discern every excellence in them! My feelings were dull compared to hers. She seemed herself to be the muse who had inspired those verses, and had tuned their lyres to infuse into the hearts of mankind the love of wisdom and virtue and the fear of the gods. How beneficent was she, how tender to my people! What care did she take to instruct them in all the finer arts, to relieve the necessities of the sick and aged, to superintend the education of children, to do my subjects every good office of kind intercession, to lay before me their wants, to mediate for those who were objects of mercy, to sue for those who deserved the favours of the Crown. And shall I banish myself for ever from such a consort? Shall I give up her society for the brutal joys of a sensual life, keeping indeed the exterior form of a man, but having lost the human soul, or at least all its noble and godlike powers? Oh, Circe, it is impossible, I can't bear the thought.

Circe. Begone; don't imagine that I ask you to stay a moment longer. The daughter of the sun is not so mean-spirited as to solicit a mortal to share her happiness with her. It is a happiness which I find you cannot enjoy. I pity and despise you. All you have said seems to me a jargon of sentiments fitter for a silly woman than a great man. Go read, and spin too, if you please, with your wife. I forbid you to remain another day in my island. You shall have a fair wind to carry you from it. After that may every storm that Neptune can raise pursue and overwhelm you. Begone, I say, quit my sight.

Ulysses. Great goddess, I obey, but remember your oath.

DIALOGUE VI. MERCURY - AN ENGLISH DUELLIST - A NORTH AMERICAN SAVAGE.

The Duellist. Mercury, Charon's boat is on the other side of the water. Allow me, before it returns, to have some conversation with the North American savage whom you brought hither with me. I never before saw one of that species. He looks very grim. Pray, sir, what is your name? I understand you speak English.

Savage. Yes, I learnt it in my childhood, having been bred for some years among the English of New York. But before I was a man I returned to my valiant countrymen, the Mohawks; and having been villainously cheated by one of yours in the sale of some rum, I never cared to have anything to do with them afterwards. Yet I took up the hatchet for them with the rest of my tribe in the late war against France, and was killed while I was out upon a scalping party. But I died very well satisfied, for my brethren were victorious, and before I was shot I had gloriously scalped seven men and five women and children. In a former war I had performed still greater exploits. My name is the Bloody Bear; it was given me to express my fierceness and valour.

Duellist. Bloody Bear, I respect you, and am much your humble servant. My name is Tom Pushwell, very well known at Arthur's. I am a gentleman by my birth, and by profession a gamester and man of honour. I have killed men in fair fighting, in honourable single combat, but don't understand cutting the throats of women and children.

Savage. Sir, that is our way of making war. Every nation has its customs. But, by the grimness of your countenance, and that hole in your breast, I presume you were killed, as I was, in some scalping party. How happened it that your enemy did not take off your scalp?

Duellist. Sir, I was killed in a duel. A friend of mine had lent me a sum of money. After two or three years, being in great want himself, he asked me to pay him. I thought his demand, which was somewhat peremptory, an affront to my honour, and sent him a challenge. We met in Hyde Park. The fellow could not fence: I was absolutely the adroitest swordsman in England, so I gave him three or four wounds; but at last he ran upon me with such impetuosity, that he put me out of my play, and I could not prevent him from whipping me through the lungs. I died the next day, as a man of honour should, without any snivelling signs of contrition or repentance; and he will follow me soon, for his surgeon has declared his wounds to be mortal. It is said that his wife is dead of grief, and that his family of seven children will be undone by his death. So I am well revenged, and that is a comfort. For my part, I had no wife. I always hated marriage.

Savage. Mercury, I won't go in a boat with that fellow. He has murdered his countryman, he has murdered his friend: I say, positively, I won't go in a boat with that fellow. I will swim over the River, I can swim like a duck.

Mercury. Swim over the Styx! it must not be done; it is against the laws of Pluto's Empire. You must go in the boat, and be quiet.

Savage. Don't tell me of laws, I am a savage. I value no laws. Talk of laws to the Englishman. There are laws in his country, and yet you see he did not regard them, for they could never allow him to kill his fellow-subject, in time of peace, because he asked him to pay a debt. I know indeed, that the English are a barbarous nation, but they can't possibly be so brutal as to make such things lawful.

Mercury. You reason well against him. But how comes it that you are so offended with murder; you, who have frequently massacred women in their sleep, and children in the cradle?

Savage. I killed none but my enemies. I never killed my own countrymen. I never killed my friend. Here, take my blanket, and let it come over in the boat, but see that the murderer does not sit upon it, or touch it. If he does, I will burn it instantly in the fire I see yonder. Farewell! I am determined to swim over the water.

Mercury. By this touch of my wand I deprive thee of all thy strength. Swim now if thou canst.

Savage. This is a potent enchanter. Restore me my strength, and I promise to obey thee.

Mercury. I restore it: but be orderly, and do as I bid you; otherwise worse will befall you.

Duellist. Mercury, leave him to me. I'll tutor him for you. Sirrah, savage, dost thou pretend to be ashamed of my company? Dost thou know I have kept the best company in England?

Savage. I know thou art a scoundrel! Not pay thy debts! kill thy friend who lent thee money for asking thee for it! Get out of my sight! I will drive thee into Styx!

Mercury. Stop! I command thee. No violence! Talk to him calmly.

Savage. I must obey thee. Well, sir, let me know what merit you had to introduce you into good company? What could you do?

Duellist. Sir, I gamed, as I told you. Besides, I kept a good table. I eat as well as any man either in England or France.

Savage. Eat! Did you ever eat the liver of a Frenchman, or his leg, or his shoulder! There is fine eating! I have eat twenty. My table was always well served. My wife was esteemed the best cook for the dressing of man's flesh in all North America. You will not pretend to compare your eating with mine?

Duellist. I danced very finely.

Savage. I'll dance with thee for thy ears: I can dance all day long. I can dance the war-dance with more spirit than any man of my nation. Let us see thee begin it. How thou standest like a post! Has Mercury struck thee with his enfeebling rod? or art thou ashamed to let us see how awkward thou art? If he would permit me, I would teach thee to dance in a way that thou hast never yet learnt. But what else canst thou do, thou bragging rascal?

Duellist. O heavens! must I bear this? What can I do with this fellow? I have neither sword nor pistol. And his shade seems to be twice as strong as mine.

Mercury. You must answer his questions. It was your own desire to have a conversation with him. He is not well bred; but he will tell you some truths which you must necessarily hear, when you come before Rhadamanthus. He asked you what you could do besides eating and dancing.

Duellist. I sang very agreeably.

Savage. Let me hear you sing your "Death Song" or the "War Whoop." I challenge you to sing. Come, begin. The fellow is mute. Mercury, this is a liar; he has told us nothing but lies. Let me pull out his tongue.

Duellist. The lie given me! and, alas, I dare not resent it. What an indelible disgrace to the family of the Pushwells! This indeed is damnation.

Mercury. Here, Charon, take these two savages to your care. How far the barbarism of the Mohawk will excuse his horrid acts I leave Minos to judge. But what can be said for the other, for the Englishman? The custom of duelling? A bad excuse at the best! but here it cannot avail. The spirit that urged him to draw his sword against his friend is not that of honour; it is the spirit of the furies, and to them he must go.

Savage. If he is to be punished for his wickedness, turn him over to me; I perfectly understand the art of tormenting. Sirrah, I begin my work with this kick on your breech.

Duellist. Oh my honour, my honour, to what infamy art thou fallen!

DIALOGUE VII. PLINY THE ELDER - PLINY THE YOUNGER.

Pliny the Elder. The account that you give me, nephew, of your behaviour amidst the tenors and perils that accompanied the first eruption of Vesuvius does not please me much. There was more of vanity in it than of true magnanimity. Nothing is great that is unnatural and affected. When the earth was shaking beneath you, when the whole heaven was darkened with sulphurous clouds, when all Nature seemed falling into its final destruction, to be reading Livy and making extracts was an absurd affectation. To meet danger with courage is manly, but to be insensible of it is brutal stupidity; and to pretend insensibility where it cannot be supposed is ridiculous falseness. When you afterwards refused to leave your aged mother and save yourself without her, you indeed acted nobly. It was also becoming a Roman to keep up her spirits amidst all the horrors of that tremendous scene by showing yourself undismayed; but the real merit and glory of this part of your behaviour is sunk by the other, which gives an air of ostentation and vanity to the whole.

Pliny the Younger. That vulgar minds should consider my attention to my studies in such a conjuncture as unnatural and affected, I should not much wonder; but that you would blame it as such I did not apprehend, you, whom no business could separate from the muses; you, who approached nearer to the fiery storm, and died by the suffocating heat of the vapour.

Pliny the Elder. I died in doing my duty. Let me recall to your remembrance all the particulars, and then you shall judge yourself on the difference of your behaviour and mine. I was the Prefect of the Roman fleet, which then lay at Misenum. On the first account I received of the very unusual cloud that appeared in the air I ordered a vessel to carry me out to some distance from the shore that I might the better observe the phenomenon, and endeavour to discover its nature and cause. This I did as a philosopher, and it was a curiosity proper and natural to an inquisitive mind. I offered to take you with me, and surely you should have gone; for Livy might have been read at any other time, and such spectacles are not frequent. When I came out from my house, I found all the inhabitants of Misenum flying to the sea. That I might assist them, and all others who dwelt on the coast, I immediately commanded the whole fleet to put out, and sailed with it all round the Bay of Naples, steering particularly to those parts of the shore where the danger was greatest, and from whence the affrighted people were endeavouring to escape with the most trepidation. Thus I happily preserved some thousands of lives, noting at the same time, with an unshaken composure and freedom of mind, the several phenomena of the eruption. Towards night, as we approached to the foot of Mount Vesuvius, our galleys were covered with ashes, the showers of which grew continually hotter and hotter; then pumice stones and burnt and broken pyrites began to fall on our heads, and we were stopped by the obstacles which the ruins of the volcano had suddenly formed, by falling into the sea and almost filling it up, on that part of the coast. I then commanded my pilot to steer to the villa of my friend Pomponianus, which, you know, was situated in the inmost recess of the bay. The wind was very favourable to carry me thither, but would not allow him to put off from the shore, as he was desirous to have done. We were, therefore, constrained to pass the night in his house. The family watched, and I slept till the heaps of pumice stones, which incessantly fell from the clouds that had by this time been impelled to that side of the bay, rose so high in the area of the apartment I lay in, that if I had stayed any longer I could not have got out; and the earthquakes were so violent as to threaten every moment the fall of the house. We, therefore, thought it more safe to go into the open air, guarding our heads as well as we were able with pillows tied upon them. The wind continuing contrary, and the sea very rough, we all remained on the shore, till the descent of a sulphurous and fiery vapour suddenly oppressed my weak lungs and put an end to my life. In all this I hope that I acted as the duty of my station required, and with true magnanimity. But on this occasion, and in many other parts of your conduct, I must say, my dear nephew, there was a mixture of vanity blended with your virtue which impaired and disgraced it. Without that you would have been one of the worthiest men whom Rome has ever produced, for none excelled you in sincere integrity of heart and greatness of sentiments. Why would you lose the substance of glory by seeking the shadow? Your eloquence had, I think, the same fault as your manners; it was generally too affected. You professed to make Cicero your guide and pattern; but when one reads his Panegyric upon Julius Caesar, in his Oration for Marcellus, and yours upon Trajan, the first seems the genuine language of truth and Nature, raised and dignified with all the majesty of the most sublime oratory; the latter appears the harangue of a florid rhetorician, more desirous to shine and to set off his own wit than to extol the great man whose virtues he was praising.

Pliny the Younger. I will not question your judgment either of my life or my writings; they might both have been better if I had not been too solicitous to render them perfect. It is, perhaps, some excuse for the affectation of my style that it was the fashion of the age in which I wrote. Even the eloquence of Tacitus, however nervous and sublime, was not unaffected. Mine, indeed, was more diffuse, and the ornaments of it were more tawdry; but his laboured conciseness, the constant glow of his diction, and pointed brilliancy of his sentences, were no less unnatural. One principal cause of this I suppose to have been that, as we despaired of excelling the two great masters of oratory, Cicero and Livy, in their own manner, we took up another, which to many appeared more shining, and gave our compositions a more original air; but it is mortifying to me to say much on this subject. Permit me, therefore, to resume the contemplation of that on which our conversation turned before. What a direful calamity was the eruption of Vesuvius, which you have been describing?

Don't you remember the beauty of that fine coast, and of the mountain itself, before it was torn with the violence of those internal fires, that forced their way through its surface. The foot of it was covered with cornfields and rich meadows, interspersed with splendid villas and magnificent towns; the sides of it were clothed with the best vines in Italy. How quick, how unexpected, how terrible was the change! All was at once overwhelmed with ashes, cinders, broken rocks, and fiery torrents, presenting to the eye the most dismal scene of horror and desolation!

Pliny the Elder. You paint it very truly. But has it never occurred to your philosophical mind that this change is a striking emblem of that which must happen, by the natural course of things, to every rich, luxurious state? While the inhabitants of it are sunk in voluptuousness, while all is smiling around them, and they imagine that no evil, no danger is nigh, the latent seeds of destruction are fermenting within; till, breaking out on a sudden, they lay waste all their opulence, all their boasted delights, and leave them a sad monument of the fatal effects of internal tempests and convulsions.

DIALOGUE VIII. FERNANDO CORTEZ - WILLIAM PENN.

Cortez. Is it possible, William Penn, that you should seriously compare your glory with mine? The planter of a small colony in North America presume to vie with the conqueror of the great Mexican Empire?

Penn. Friend, I pretend to no glory, the Lord preserve me from it. All glory is His; but this I say, that I was His instrument in a more glorious work than that performed by thee, incomparably more glorious.

Cortez. Dost thou not know, William Penn, that with less than six hundred Spanish foot, eighteen horse, and a few small pieces of cannon, I fought and defeated innumerable armies of very brave men; dethroned an emperor who had been raised to the throne by his valour, and excelled all his countrymen in the science of war, as much as they excelled all the rest of the West Indian nations? That I made him my prisoner in his own capital; and, after he had been deposed and slain by his subjects, vanquished and took Guatimozin, his successor, and accomplished my conquest of the whole empire of Mexico, which I loyally annexed to the Spanish Crown? Dost thou not know that, in doing these wonderful acts, I showed as much courage as Alexander the Great, as much prudence as Caesar? That by my policy I ranged under my banners the powerful commonwealth of Tlascala, and brought them to assist me in subduing the Mexicans, though with the loss of their own beloved independence? and that, to consummate my glory, when the Governor of Cuba, Velasquez, would have taken my command from me and sacrificed me to his envy and jealousy, I drew from him all his forces and joined them to my own, showing myself as superior to all other Spaniards as I was to the Indians?

Penn. I know very well that thou wast as fierce as a lion and as subtle as a serpent. The devil perhaps may place thee as high in his black list of heroes as Alexander or Caesar. It is not my business to interfere with him in settling thy rank. But hark thee, friend Cortez. What right hadst thou, or had the King of Spain himself, to the Mexican Empire? Answer me that, if thou canst.

Cortez. The Pope gave it to my master.

Penn. The devil offered to give our Lord all the kingdoms of the earth, and I suppose the Pope, as his vicar, gave thy master this; in return for which he fell down and worshipped him, like an idolater as he was. But suppose the high priest of Mexico had taken it into his head to give Spain to Montezuma, would his grant have been good?

Cortez. These are questions of casuistry which it is not the business of a soldier to decide. We leave that to gownsmen. But pray, Mr. Penn, what right had you to the province you settled?

Penn. An honest right of fair purchase. We gave the native savages some things they wanted, and they in return gave us lands they did not want. All was amicably agreed on, not a drop of blood shed to stain our acquisition.

Cortez. I am afraid there was a little fraud in the purchase. Thy followers, William Penn, are said to think cheating in a quiet and sober way no mortal sin.

Penn. The saints are always calumniated by the ungodly. But it was a sight which an angel might contemplate with delight to behold the colony I settled! To see us living with the Indians like innocent lambs, and taming the ferocity of their barbarous manners by the gentleness of ours! To see the whole country, which before was an uncultivated wilderness, rendered as fertile and fair as the garden of God! O Fernando Cortez, Fernando Cortez! didst thou leave the great empire of Mexico in that state? No, thou hadst turned those delightful and populous regions into a desert, a desert flooded with blood. Dost thou not remember that most infernal scene when the noble Emperor Guatimozin was stretched out by thy soldiers upon hot burning coals to make him discover into what part of the lake of Mexico he had thrown the royal treasures? Are not his groans ever sounding in the ears of thy conscience? Do not they rend thy hard heart, and strike thee with more horror than the yells of the furies?

Cortez. Alas! I was not present when that dire act was done. Had I been there I would have forbidden it. My nature was mild.

Penn. Thou wast the captain of that band of robbers who did this horrid deed. The advantage they had drawn from thy counsels and conduct enabled them to commit it; and thy skill saved them afterwards from the vengeance that was due to so enormous a crime. The enraged Mexicans would have properly punished them for it, if they had not had thee for their general, thou lieutenant of Satan.

Cortez. The saints I find can rail, William Penn. But how do you hope to preserve this admirable colony which you have settled? Your people, you tell me, live like innocent lambs. Are there no wolves in North America to devour those lambs? But if the Americans should continue in perpetual peace with all your successors there, the French will not. Are the inhabitants of Pennsylvania to make war against them with prayers and preaching? If so, that garden of God which you say you have planted will undoubtedly be their prey, and they will take from you your property, your laws, and your religion.

Penn. The Lord's will be done. The Lord will defend us against the rage of our enemies if it be His good pleasure.

Cortez. Is this the wisdom of a great legislator? I have heard some of your countrymen compare you to Solon. Did Solon, think you, give laws to a people, and leave those laws and that people at the mercy of every invader? The first business of legislature is to provide a military strength that may defend the whole system. If a house is built in a land of robbers, without a gate to shut or a bolt or bar to secure it, what avails it how well-proportioned or how commodious the architecture of it may be? Is it richly furnished within? the more it will tempt the hands of violence and of rapine to seize its wealth. The world, William Penn, is all a land of robbers. Any state or commonwealth erected therein must be well fenced and secured by good military institutions; or, the happier it is in all other respects, the greater will be its danger, the more speedy its destruction. Perhaps the neighbouring

English colonies may for a while protect yours; but that precarious security cannot always preserve you. Your plan of government must be changed, or your colony will be lost. What I have said is also applicable to Great Britain itself. If an increase of its wealth be not accompanied with an increase of its force that wealth will become the prey of some of the neighbouring nations, in which the martial spirit is more prevalent than the commercial. And whatever praise may be due to its civil institutions, if they are not guarded by a wise system of military policy, they will be found of no value, being unable to prevent their own dissolution.

Penn. These are suggestions of human wisdom. The doctrines I held were inspired; they came from above.

Cortez. It is blasphemy to say that any folly could come from the Fountain of Wisdom. Whatever is inconsistent with the great laws of Nature and with the necessary state of human society cannot possibly have been inspired by God. Self-defence is as necessary to nations as to men. And shall particulars have a right which nations have not? True religion, William Penn, is the perfection of reason; fanaticism is the disgrace, the destruction of reason.

Penn. Though what thou sayest should be true, it does not come well from thy mouth. A Papist talk of reason! Go to the Inquisition and tell them of reason and the great laws of Nature. They will broil thee, as thy soldiers broiled the unhappy Guatimozin. Why dost thou turn pale? Is it the name of the Inquisition, or the name of Guatimozin, that troubles and affrights thee? O wretched man! who madest thyself a voluntary instrument to carry into a new-discovered world that hellish tribunal? Tremble and shake when thou thinkest that every murder the Inquisitors have committed, every torture they have inflicted on the innocent Indians, is originally owing to thee. Thou must answer to God for all their inhumanity, for all their injustice. What wouldst thou give to part with the renown of thy conquests, and to have a conscience as pure and undisturbed as mine?

Cortez. I feel the force of thy words; they pierce me like daggers. I can never, never be happy, while I retain any memory of the ills I have caused. Yet I thought I did right. I thought I laboured to advance the glory of God and propagate, in the remotest parts of the earth, His holy religion. He will be merciful to well designing and pious error. Thou also wilt have need of that gracious indulgence, though not, I own, so much as I.

Penn. Ask thy heart whether ambition was not thy real motive and zeal the pretence?

Cortez. Ask thine whether thy zeal had no worldly views and whether thou didst believe all the nonsense of the sect, at the head of which thou wast pleased to become a legislator. Adieu. Self-examination requires retirement.

DIALOGUE IX. MARCUS PORTIUS CATO - MESSALLA CORVINUS.

Cato. Oh, Messalla! is it then possible that what some of our countrymen tell me should be true? Is it possible that you could live the courtier of Octavius; that you could accept of employments and honours from him, from the tyrant of your country; you, the brave, the noble-minded, the virtuous Messalla; you, whom I remember, my son-in-law Brutus has frequently extolled as the most promising youth in Rome, tutored by philosophy, trained up in arms, scorning all those soft, effeminate pleasures that reconcile men to an easy and indolent servitude, fit for all the roughest tasks of honour and virtue, fit to live or to die a free man?

Messalla. Marcus Cato, I revere both your life and your death; but the last, permit me to tell you, did no good to your country, and the former would have done more if you could have mitigated a little the sternness of your virtue, I will not say of your pride. For my own part, I adhered with constant integrity and unwearied zeal to the Republic, while the Republic existed. I fought for her at Philippi under the only commander, who, if he had conquered, would have conquered for her, not for himself. When he was dead I saw that nothing remained to my country but the choice of a master. I chose the best.

Cato. The best! What! a man who had broken all laws, who had violated all trusts, who had led the armies of the Commonwealth against Antony, and then joined with him and that sottish traitor Lepidus, to set up a triumvirate more execrable by far than either of the former; who shed the best blood in Rome by an inhuman proscription, murdered even his own guardian, murdered Cicero, to whose confidence, too improvidently given, he owed all his power? Was this the master you chose? Could you bring your tongue to give him the name of Augustus? Could you stoop to beg consulships and triumphs from him? Oh, shame to virtue! Oh, degeneracy of Rome! To what infamy are her sons, her noblest sons, fallen. The thought of it pains me more than the wound that I died of; it stabs my soul.

Messalla. Moderate, Cato, the vehemence of your indignation. There has always been too much passion mixed with your virtue. The enthusiasm you are possessed with is a noble one, but it disturbs your judgment. Hear me with patience, and with the tranquillity that becomes a philosopher. It is true that Octavius had done all you have said; but it is no less true that, in our circumstances, he was the best master Rome could choose. His mind was fitted by nature for empire. His understanding was clear and strong. His passions were cool, and under the absolute command of his reason. His name gave him an authority over the troops and the people which no other Roman could possess in an equal degree. He used that authority to restrain the excesses of both, which it was no longer in the power of the Senate to repress, nor of any other general or magistrate in the state. He restored discipline in our armies, the first means of salvation, without which no legal government could have been formed or supported. He avoided all odious and invidious names. He maintained and respected those which time and long habits had endeared to the Roman people. He permitted a generous liberty of speech. He treated the nobles of Pompey's party as well as those of his father's, if they did not themselves, for factious purposes, keep up the distinction. He formed a plan of government, moderate, decent, respectable, which left the senate its majesty, and some of its power. He restored vigour and spirit to the laws; he made new and good ones for the reformation of manners; he enforced their execution; he governed the empire with lenity, justice, and glory; he humbled the pride of the Parthians; he broke the fierceness of the barbarous nations; he gave to his country, exhausted and languishing with the great loss of blood which she had sustained in the course of so many civil wars, the blessing of peace, a blessing which was become so necessary for her, that without it she could enjoy no other. In doing these things I acknowledge he had my assistance. I am prouder of it, and I think I can justify myself more effectually to my country, than if I had died by my own hand at Philippi. Believe me, Cato, it is better to do some good than to project a great deal. A little practical virtue is of more use to society than the most sublime theory, or the best principles of government ill applied.

Cato. Yet I must think it was beneath the character of Messalla to join in supporting a government which, though coloured and mitigated, was still a tyranny. Had you not better have gone into a voluntary exile, where you would not have seen the face of the tyrant, and where you might have quietly practised those private virtues which are all that the gods require from good men in certain situations?

Messalla. No; I did much more good by continuing at Rome. Had Augustus required of me anything base, anything servile, I would have gone into exile, I would have died, rather than do it. But he respected my virtue, he respected my dignity; he treated me as well as Agrippa, or as Maecenas, with this distinction alone, that he never employed my sword but against foreign nations, or the old enemies of the republic.

Cato. It must, I own, have been a pleasure to be employed against Antony, that monster of vice, who plotted the ruin of liberty, and the raising of himself to sovereign power, amidst the riot of bacchanals, and in the embraces of harlots, who, when he had attained to that power, delivered it up to a lascivious queen, and would have made an Egyptian strumpet the mistress of Rome, if the Battle of Actium had not saved us from that last of misfortunes.

Messalla. In that battle I had a considerable share. So I had in encouraging the liberal arts and sciences, which Augustus protected. Under his judicious patronage the muses made Rome their capital seat. It would have pleased you to have known Virgil, Horace, Tibullus, Ovid, Livy, and many more, whose names will be illustrious to all generations.

Cato. I understand you, Messalla. Your Augustus and you, after the ruin of our liberty, made Rome a Greek city, an academy of fine wits, another Athens under the government of Demetrius Phalareus. I had much rather have seen her under Fabricius and Curius, and her other honest old consuls, who could not read.

Messalla. Yet to these writers she will owe as much of her glory as she did to those heroes. I could say more, a great deal more, on the happiness of the mild dominion of Augustus. I might even add, that the vast extent of the empire, the factions of the nobility, and the corruption of the people, which no laws under the ordinary magistrates of the state were able to restrain, seemed necessarily to require some change in the government; that Cato himself, had he remained upon earth, could have done us no good, unless he would have yielded to become our prince. But I see you consider me as a deserter from the republic, and an apologist for a tyrant. I, therefore, leave you to the company of those ancient Romans, for whose society you were always much fitter than for that of your contemporaries. Cato should have lived with Fabricius and Curius, not with Pompey and Caesar.

DIALOGUE X. CHRISTINA, Queen Of Sweden, Chancellor Oxenstiern.

Christina. You seem to avoid me, Oxenstiern; and, now we are met, you don't pay me the reverence that is due to your queen! Have you forgotten that I was your sovereign?

Oxenstiern. I am not your subject here, madam; but you have forgotten that you yourself broke that bond, and freed me from my allegiance, many years before you died, by abdicating the crown, against my advice and the inclination of your people. Reverence here is paid only to virtue.

Christina. I see you would mortify me if it were in your power for acting against your advice. But my fame does not depend upon your judgment. All Europe admired the greatness of my mind in resigning a crown to dedicate myself entirely to the love of the sciences and the fine arts; things of which you had no taste in barbarous Sweden, the realm of Goths and Vandals.

Oxenstiern. There is hardly any mind too great for a crown, but there are many too little. Are you sure, madam, it was magnanimity that caused you to fly from the government of a kingdom which your ancestors, and particularly your heroic father Gustavus, had ruled with so much glory?

Christina. Am I sure of it? Yes; and to confirm my own judgment, I have that of many learned men and beaux esprits of all countries, who have celebrated my action as the perfection of heroism.

Oxenstiern. Those beaux esprits judged according to their predominant passion. I have heard young ladies express their admiration of Mark Antony for heroically leaving his fleet at the Battle of Actium to follow his mistress. Your passion for literature had the same effect upon you. But why did not you indulge it in a manner more becoming your birth and rank? Why did not you bring the muses to Sweden, instead of deserting that kingdom to seek them in Rome? For a prince to encourage and protect arts and sciences, and more especially to instruct an illiterate people and inspire them with knowledge, politeness, and fine taste is indeed an act of true greatness.

Christina. The Swedes were too gross to be refined by any culture which I could have given to their dull, their half-frozen souls. Wit and genius require the influence of a more southern climate.

Oxenstiern. The Swedes too gross! No, madam, not even the Russians are too gross to be refined if they had a prince to instruct them.

Christina. It was too tedious a work for the vivacity of my temper to polish bears into men. I should have died of the spleen before I had made any proficiency in it. My desire was to shine among those who were qualified to judge of my talents. At Paris, at Rome I had the glory of showing the French and Italian wits that the North could produce one not inferior to them. They beheld me with wonder. The homage I had received in my palace at Stockholm was paid to my dignity. That which I drew from the French and Roman academies was paid to my talents. How much more glorious, how much more delightful to an elegant and rational mind was the latter than the former! Could you once have felt the joy, the transport of my heart, when I saw the greatest authors and all the celebrated artists in the most learned and civilised countries of Europe bringing their works to me and submitting the merit of them to my decisions; when I saw the philosophers, the rhetoricians, the poets making my judgment the standard of their reputation, you would not wonder that I preferred the empire of wit to any other empire.

Oxenstiern. O great Gustavus! my ever-honoured, my adored master! O greatest of kings, greatest in valour, in virtue, in wisdom, with what indignation must thy soul, enthroned in heaven, have looked down on thy unworthy, thy degenerate daughter! With what shame must thou have seen her rambling about from court to court deprived of her royal dignity, debased into a pedant, a witling, a smatterer in sculpture and painting, reduced to beg or buy flattery from each needy rhetorician or hireling poet! I weep to think on this stain, this dishonourable stain, to thy illustrious blood! And yet, would to God! would to God! this was all the pollution it has suffered!

Christina. Darest thou, Oxenstiern, impute any blemish to my honour?

Oxenstiern. Madam, the world will scarce respect the frailties of queens when they are on their thrones, much less when they have voluntarily degraded themselves to the level of the vulgar. And if scandalous tongues have unjustly aspersed their fame, the way to clear it is not by an assassination.

Christina. Oh! that I were alive again, and restored to my throne, that I might punish the insolence of this hoary traitor! But, see! he leaves me, he turns his back upon me with cool contempt! Alas! do I not deserve this scorn? In spite of myself I must confess that I do. O vanity, how short-lived are the pleasures thou bestowest! I was thy votary. Thou wast the god for whom I changed my religion. For thee I forsook my country and my throne. What compensation have I gained for all these sacrifices so lavishly, so imprudently made? Some puffs of incense from authors who thought their flattery due to the rank I had held, or hoped to advance themselves by my recommendation, or, at best, over-rated my passion for literature, and praised me to raise the value of those talents with which they were endowed. But in the esteem of wise men I stand very low, and their esteem alone is the true measure of glory. Nothing, I perceive, can give the mind a lasting joy but the consciousness of having performed our duty in that station which it has pleased the Divine Providence to assign to us. The glory of virtue is solid and eternal. All other will fade away like a thin vapoury cloud, on which the casual glance of some faint beams of light has superficially imprinted their weak and transient colours.

DIALOGUE XI. TITUS VESPASIANUS - PUBLIUS CORNELIUS SCIPIO AFRICANUS.

Titus. No, Scipio, I can't give place to you in this. In other respects I acknowledge myself your inferior, though I was Emperor of Rome and you only her consul. I think your triumph over Carthage more glorious than mine over Judaea. But in that I gained over love I must esteem myself superior to you, though your generosity with regard to the fair Celtiberian, your captive, has been celebrated so highly.

Scipio. Fame has been, then, unjust to your merit, for little is said of the continence of Titus, but mine has been the favourite topic of eloquence in every age and country.

Titus. It has; and in particular your great historian Livy has poured forth all the ornaments of his admirable rhetoric to embellish and dignify that part of your story. I had a great historian too, Cornelius Tacitus; but either from the brevity which he affected in writing, or from the severity of his nature, which never having felt the passion of love, thought the subduing of it too easy a victory to deserve great encomiums, he has bestowed but three lines upon my parting with Berenice, which cost me more pain and greater efforts of mind than the conquest of Jerusalem.

Scipio. I wish to hear from yourself the history of that parting, and what could make it so hard and painful to you.

Titus. While I served in Palestine under the auspices of my father, Vespasian, I became acquainted with Berenice, sister to King Agrippa, and who was herself a queen in one of those Eastern countries. She was the most beautiful woman in Asia, but she had graces more irresistible still than her beauty. She had all the insinuation and wit of Cleopatra, without her coquetry. I loved her, and was beloved; she loved my person, not my greatness. Her tenderness, her fidelity so inflamed my passion for her that I gave her a promise of marriage.

Scipio. What do I hear? A Roman senator promise to marry a queen!

Titus. I expected, Scipio, that your ears would be offended with the sound of such a match. But consider that Rome was very different in my time from Rome in yours. The ferocious pride of our ancient republican senators had bent itself to the obsequious complaisance of a court. Berenice made no doubt, and I flattered myself that it would not be inflexible in this point alone. But we thought it necessary to defer the completion of our wishes till the death of my father. On that event the Roman Empire and (what I knew she valued more) my hand became due to her, according to my engagements.

Scipio. The Roman Empire due to a Syrian queen! Oh, Rome, how art thou fallen! Accursed be the memory of Octavius Caesar, who by oppressing its liberty so lowered the majesty of the republic, that a brave and virtuous Roman, in whom was vested all the power of that mighty state, could entertain such a thought! But did you find the senate and people so servile, so lost to all sense of their honour and dignity, as to affront the great genius of imperial Rome and the eyes of her tutelary gods, the eyes of Jupiter Capitolinus, with the sight of a queen, an Asiatic queen, on the throne of the Caesars?

Titus. I did not. They judged of it as you, Scipio, judge; they detested, they disdained it. In vain did I urge to some particular friends, who represented to me the sense of the Senate and people, that a Messalina, a Poppaea, were a much greater dishonour to the throne of the Caesars than a virtuous foreign princess. Their prejudices were unconquerable; I saw it would be impossible for me to remove them. But I might have used my authority to silence their murmurs. A liberal donative to the soldiers, by whom I was fondly beloved, would have secured their fidelity, and consequently would have forced the Senate and people to yield to my inclination. Berenice knew this, and with tears implored me not to sacrifice her happiness and my own to an unjust prepossession. Shall I own it to you, Publius? My heart not only pitied her, but acknowledged the truth and solidity of her reasons. Yet so much did I abhor the idea of tyranny, so much respect did I pay to the sentiments of my subjects, that I determined to separate myself from her for ever, rather than force either the laws or the prejudices of Rome to submit to my will.

Scipio. Give me thy hand, noble Titus. Thou wast worthy of the empire, and Scipio Africanus honours thy virtue.

Titus. My virtue can have no greater reward from the approbation of man. But, O Scipio, think what anguish my heart must have felt when I took that resolution, and when I communicated it to my dear, my unhappy Berenice. You saw the struggle of Masinissa, when you forced him to give up his beloved Sophonisba. Mine was a harder conflict. She had abandoned him to marry the King of Numidia. He knew that her ruling passion was ambition, not love. He could not rationally esteem her when she quitted a husband whom she had ruined, who had lost his crown and his liberty in the cause of her country and for her sake, to give her person to him, the capital foe of that unfortunate husband. He must, in spite of his passion, have thought her a perfidious, a detestable woman. But I esteemed Berenice; she deserved my esteem. I was certain she would not have accepted the empire from any other hand; and had I been a private man she would have raised me to her throne. Yet I had the fortitude, I ought, perhaps, to say the hardness of heart, to bid her depart from my sight; depart for ever! What, O Publius, was your conquest over yourself, in giving back to her betrothed lover the Celtiberian captive compared to this? Indeed, that was no conquest. I will not so dishonour the virtue of Scipio as to think he could feel any struggle with himself on that account. A woman engaged to another, engaged by affection as well as vows, let her have been ever so beautiful, could raise in your heart no sentiments but compassion and friendship. To have violated her would have been an act of brutality, which none but another Tarquin could have committed. To have detained her from her husband would have been cruel. But where love is mutual, where the object beloved suffers more in the separation than you do yourself, to part with her is indeed a struggle. It is the hardest sacrifice a good heart can make to its duty.

Scipio. I acknowledge that it is, and yield you the palm. But I will own to you, Titus, I never knew much of the tenderness you describe. Hannibal, Carthage, Rome, the saving of my country, the subduing of its rival, these filled my thoughts, and left no room there for those effeminate passions.

I do not blame your sensibility; but when I went to the capitol to talk with Jove, I never consulted him about love affairs.

Titus. If my soul had been possessed by ambition alone, I might possibly have been a greater man than I was; but I should not have been more virtuous, nor have gained the title I preferred to that of conqueror of Judaea and Emperor of Rome, in being called the delight of humankind.

DIALOGUE XII HENRY DUKE OF GUISE - MACHIAVEL.

Guise. Avaunt! thou fiend. I abhor thy sight. I look upon thee as the original cause of my death, and of all the calamities brought upon the French nation, in my father's time and my own.

Machiavel. I the cause of your death! You surprise me!

Guise. Yes. Your pernicious maxims of policy, imported from Florence with Catherine of Medicis, your wicked disciple, produced in France such a government, such dissimulation, such perfidy, such violent, ruthless counsels, as threw that whole kingdom into the utmost confusion, and ended my life, even in the palace of my sovereign, by the swords of assassins.

Machiavel. Whoever may have a right to complain of my policy, you, sir, have not. You owed your greatness to it, and your deviating from it was the real cause of your death. If it had not been for the assassination of Admiral Coligni and the massacre of the Huguenots, the strength and power which the conduct of so able a chief would have given to that party, after the death of your father, its most dangerous enemy, would have been fatal to your house; nor could you, even with all the advantage you drew from that great stroke of royal policy, have acquired the authority you afterwards rose to in the kingdom of France; but by pursuing my maxims, by availing yourself of the specious name of religion to serve the secret purposes of your ambition, and by suffering no restraint of fear or conscience, not even the guilt of exciting a civil war, to check the necessary progress of your well-concerted designs. But on the day of the barricades you most imprudently let the king escape out of Paris, when you might have slain or deposed him. This was directly against the great rule of my politics, not to stop short in rebellion or treason till the work is fully completed. And you were justly censured for it by Pope Sixtus Quintus, a more consummate politician, who said, "You ought to have known that when a subject draws his sword against his king he should throw away the scabbard." You likewise deviated from my counsels, by putting yourself in the power of a sovereign you had so much offended. Why would you, against all the cautions I had given, expose your life in a loyal castle to the mercy of that prince? You trusted to his fear, but fear, insulted and desperate, is often cruel. Impute therefore your death not to any fault in my maxims, but to your own folly in not having sufficiently observed them.

Guise. If neither I nor that prince had ever practised your maxims in any part of our conduct, he would have reigned many years with honour and peace, and I should have risen by my courage and talents to as high a pitch of greatness as it consisted with the duty of a subject to desire. But your instructions led us on into those crooked paths, out of which there was no retreat without great danger, nor a possibility of advancing without being detested by all mankind, and whoever is so has everything to fear from that detestation. I will give you a proof of this in the fate of a prince, who ought to have been your hero instead of Caesar Borgia, because he was incomparably a greater man, and, of all who ever lived, seems to have acted most steadily according to the rules laid down by you; I mean Richard III., King of England. He stopped at no crime that could be profitable to him; he was a dissembler, a hypocrite, a murderer in cool blood. After the death of his brother he gained the crown by cutting off, without pity, all who stood in his way. He trusted no man any further than helped his own purposes and consisted with his own safety. He liberally rewarded all services done him, but would not let the remembrance of them atone for offences or save any man from destruction who obstructed his views. Nevertheless, though his nature shrunk from no wickedness which could serve his ambition, he possessed and exercised all those virtues which you recommend to the practice of your prince. He was bold and prudent in war, just and strict in the general administration of his government, and particularly careful, by a vigorous execution of the laws, to protect the people against injuries or oppressions from the great. In all his actions and words there constantly appeared the highest concern for the honour of the nation. He was neither greedy of wealth that belonged to other men nor profuse of his own, but knew how to give and where to save. He professed a most edifying sense of religion, pretended great zeal for the reformation of manners, and was really an example of sobriety, chastity, and temperance in the whole course of his life. Nor did he shed any blood, but of those who were such obstacles in his way to dominion as could not possibly be removed by any other means. This was a prince after your heart, yet mark his end. The horror his crimes had excited in the minds of his subjects, and the detestation it produced, were so pernicious to him, that they enabled an exile, who had no right to the crown, and whose abilities were much inferior to his, to invade his realm and destroy him.

Machiavel. This example, I own, may seem to be of some weight against the truth of my system. But at the same time it demonstrates that there was nothing so new in the doctrines I published as to make it reasonable to charge me with the disorders and mischiefs which, since my time, any kingdom may have happened to suffer from the ambition of a subject or the tyranny of a prince. Human nature wants no teaching to render it wicked. In courts more especially there has been, from the first institution of monarchies, a policy practised, not less repugnant than mine to the narrow and vulgar laws of humanity and religion. Why should I be singled out as worse than other statesmen?

Guise. There have been, it must be owned, in all ages and all states, many wicked politicians; but thou art the first that ever taught the science of tyranny, reduced it to rules, and instructed his disciples how to acquire and secure it by treachery, perjuries, assassinations, proscriptions, and with a particular caution, not to be stopped in the progress of their crimes by any check of the conscience or feeling of the heart, but to push them as far as they shall judge to be necessary to their greatness and safety. It is this which has given thee a pre-eminence in guilt over all other statesmen.

Machiavel. If you had read my book with candour you would have perceived that I did not desire to render men either tyrants or rebels, but only showed, if they were so, what conduct, in such circumstances, it would be rational and expedient for them to observe.

Guise. When you were a minister of state in Florence, if any chemist or physician had published a treatise, to instruct his countrymen in the art of poisoning, and how to do it with the most certain destruction to others and security to themselves, would you have allowed him to plead in his justification that he did not desire men to poison their neighbours? But, if they would use such evil means of mending their fortunes, there could surely be no harm in letting them know what were the most effectual poisons, and by what methods they might give them without being discovered. Would you have thought it a sufficient apology for him that he had dropped in his preface, or here and there in his book, a sober exhortation against the committing of murder? Without all doubt, as a magistrate concerned for the safety of the people of Florence, you would have punished the wretch with the utmost severity, and taken great care to destroy every copy of so pernicious a book. Yet your own admired work contains a more baneful and more infernal art. It poisons states and kingdoms, and spreads its malignity, like a general pestilence, over the whole world.

Machiavel. You must acknowledge at least that my discourses on Livy are full of wise and virtuous maxims and precepts of government.

Guise. This, I think, rather aggravates than alleviates your guilt. How could you study and comment upon Livy with so acute and profound an understanding, and afterwards write a book so absolutely repugnant to all the lessons of policy taught by that sage and moral historian? How could you, who had seen the picture of virtue so amiably drawn by his hand, and who seemed yourself to be sensible of all its charms, fall in love with a fury, and set up her dreadful image as an object of worship to princes?

Machiavel. I was seduced by vanity. My heart was formed to love virtue. But I wanted to be thought a greater genius in politics than Aristotle or Plato. Vanity, sir, is a passion as strong in authors as ambition in princes, or rather it is the same passion exerting itself differently. I was a Duke of Guise in the republic of letters.

Guise. The bad influences of your guilt have reached further than mine, and been more lasting. But, Heaven be praised, your credit is at present much declining in Europe. I have been told by some shades who are lately arrived here, that the ablest statesman of his time, a king, with whose fame the world is filled, has answered your book, and confuted all the principles of it, with a noble scorn and abhorrence. I am also assured, that in England there is a great and good king, whose whole life has been a continued opposition to your evil system; who has hated all cruelty, all fraud, all falseness; whose word has been sacred, whose honour inviolate; who has made the laws of his kingdom the rules of his government, and good faith and a regard for the liberty of mankind the principles of his conduct with respect to foreign powers; who reigns more absolutely now in the hearts of his people, and does greater things by the confidence they place in him, and by the efforts they make from the generous zeal of affection, than any monarch ever did, or ever will do, by all the arts of iniquity which you recommended.

DIALOGUE XIII. VIRGIL – HORACE – MERCURY - SCALIGER THE ELDER.

Virgil. My dear Horace, your company is my greatest delight, even in the Elysian Fields. No wonder it was so when we lived together in Rome. Never had man so genteel, so agreeable, so easy a wit, or a temper so pliant to the inclinations of others in the intercourse of society. And then such integrity, such fidelity, such generosity in your nature! A soul so free from all envy, so benevolent, so sincere, so placable in its anger, so warm and constant in its affections! You were as necessary to Maecenas as he to Augustus. Your conversation sweetened to him all the cares of his ministry; your gaiety cheered his drooping spirits; and your counsels assisted him when he wanted advice. For you were capable, my dear Horace, of counselling statesmen. Your sagacity, your discretion, your secrecy, your clear judgment in all affairs, recommended you to the confidence, not of Maecenas alone, but of Augustus himself; which you nobly made use of to serve your old friends of the republican party, and to confirm both the minister and the prince in their love of mild and moderate measures, yet with a severe restraint of licentiousness, the most dangerous enemy to the whole commonwealth under any form of government.

Horace. To be so praised by Virgil would have put me in Elysium while I was alive. But I know your modesty will not suffer me, in return for these encomiums, to speak of your character. Supposing it as perfect as your poems, you would think, as you did of them, that it wanted correction.

Virgil. Don't talk of my modesty. How much greater was yours, when you disclaimed the name of a poet, you whose odes are so noble, so harmonious, so sublime!

Horace. I felt myself too inferior to the dignity of that name.

Virgil. I think you did like Augustus, when he refused to accept the title of king, but kept all the power with which it was ever attended. Even in your Epistles and Satires, where the poet was concealed, as much as he could be, you may properly be compared to a prince in disguise, or in his hours of familiarity with his intimate friends: the pomp and majesty were let drop, but the greatness remained.

Horace. Well, I will not contradict you; and, to say the truth, I should do it with no very good grace, because in some of my Odes I have not spoken so modestly of my own poetry as in my Epistles. But to make you know your pre-eminence over me and all writers of Latin verse, I will carry you to Quintilian, the best of all Roman critics, who will tell you in what rank you ought to be placed.

Virgil. I fear his judgment of me was biassed by your commendation. But who is this shade that Mercury is conducting? I never saw one that stalked with so much pride, or had such ridiculous arrogance expressed in his looks!

Horace. They come towards us. Hail, Mercury! What is this stranger with you?

Mercury. His name is Julius Caesar Scaliger, and he is by profession a critic.

Horace. Julius Caesar Scaliger! He was, I presume, a dictator in criticism.

Mercury. Yes, and he has exercised his sovereign power over you.

Horace. I will not presume to oppose it. I had enough of following Brutus at Philippi.

Mercury. Talk to him a little. He'll amuse you. I brought him to you on purpose.

Horace. Virgil, do you accost him. I can't do it with proper gravity. I shall laugh in his face.

Virgil. Sir, may I ask for what reason you cast your eyes so superciliously upon Horace and me? I don't remember that Augustus ever looked down upon us with such an air of superiority when we were his subjects.

Scaliger. He was only a sovereign over your bodies, and owed his power to violence and usurpation. But I have from Nature an absolute dominion over the wit of all authors, who are subjected to me as the greatest of critics or hypercritics.

Virgil. Your jurisdiction, great sir, is very extensive. And what judgments have you been pleased to pass upon us?

Scaliger. Is it possible you should be ignorant of my decrees? I have placed you, Virgil, above Homer, whom I have shown to be

Virgil. Hold, sir. No blasphemy against my master.

Horace. But what have you said of me?

Scaliger. I have said that I had rather have written the little dialogue between you and Lydia than have been made king of Arragon.

Horace. If we were in the other world you should give me the kingdom, and take both the ode and the lady in return. But did you always pronounce so favourably for us?

Scaliger. Send for my works and read them. Mercury will bring them to you with the first learned ghost that arrives here from Europe. There is instruction for you in them. I tell you of your faults. But it was my whim to commend that little ode, and I never do things by halves. When I give praise, I give it liberally, to show my royal bounty. But I generally blame, to exert all the vigour of my censorian power, and keep my subjects in awe.

Horace. You did not confine your sovereignty to poets; you exercised it, no doubt, over all other writers.

Scaliger. I was a poet, a philosopher, a statesman, an orator, an historian, a divine without doing the drudgery of any of these, but only censuring those who did, and showing thereby the superiority of my genius over them all.

Horace. A short way, indeed, to universal fame! And I suppose you were very peremptory in your decisions?

Scaliger. Peremptory! ay. If any man dared to contradict my opinions I called him a dunce, a rascal, a villain, and frightened him out of his wits.

Virgil. But what said others to this method of disputation?

Scaliger. They generally believed me because of the confidence of my assertions, and thought I could not be so insolent or so angry if I was not absolutely sure of being in the right. Besides, in my controversies, I had a great help from the language in which I wrote. For one can scold and call names with a much better grace in Latin than in French or any tame modern tongue.

Horace. Have not I heard that you pretended to derive your descent from the princes of Verona?

Scaliger. Pretended! Do you presume to deny it?

Horace. Not I, indeed. Genealogy is not my science. If you should claim to descend in a direct line from King Midas I would not dispute it.

Virgil. I wonder, Scaliger, that you stooped to so low an ambition. Was it not greater to reign over all Mount Parnassus than over a petty state in Italy?

Scaliger. You say well. I was too condescending to the prejudices of vulgar opinion. The ignorant multitude imagine that a prince is a greater man than a critic. Their folly made me desire to claim kindred with the Scalas of Verona.

Horace. Pray, Mercury, how do you intend to dispose of this august person? You can't think it proper to let him remain with us. He must be placed with the demigods; he must go to Olympus.

Mercury. Be not afraid. He shall not trouble you long. I brought him hither to divert you with the sight of an animal you never had seen, and myself with your surprise. He is the chief of all the modern critics, the most renowned captain of that numerous and dreadful band. Whatever you may think of him, I can seriously assure you that before he went mad he had good parts and great learning. But I will now explain to you the original cause of the absurdities he has uttered. His mind was formed in such a manner that, like some perspective glasses, it either diminished or magnified all objects too much; but, above all others, it magnified the good man to himself. This made him so proud that it turned his brain. Now I have had my sport with him, I think it will be charity to restore him to his senses, or rather to bestow what Nature denied him, a sound judgment. Come hither, Scaliger. By this touch of my Caduceus I give thee power to see things as they are, and, among others, thyself. Look, gentlemen, how his countenance is fallen in a moment! Hear what he says. He is talking to himself.

Scaliger. Bless me! with what persons have I been discoursing? With Virgil and Horace! How could I venture to open my lips in their presence? Good Mercury, I beseech you let me retire from a company for which I am very unfit. Let me go and hide my head in the deepest shade of that grove which I see in the valley. After I have performed a penance there, I will crawl on my knees to the feet of those illustrious shades, and beg them to see me burn my impertinent books of criticism in the fiery billows of Phlegethon with my own hands.

Mercury. They will both receive thee into favour. This mortification of truly knowing thyself is a sufficient atonement for thy former presumption.

DIALOGUE XIV. BOILEAU - POPE.

Boileau. Mr. Pope, you have done me great honour. I am told that you made me your model in poetry, and walked on Parnassus in the same paths which I had trod.

Pope. We both followed Horace, but in our manner of imitation, and in the turn of our natural genius, there was, I believe, much resemblance. We both were too irritable and too easily hurt by offences, even from the lowest of men. The keen edge of our wit was frequently turned against those whom it was more a shame to contend with than an honour to vanquish.

Boileau. Yes. But in general we were the champions of good morals, good sense, and good learning. If our love of these was sometimes heated into anger against those who offended them no less than us, is that anger to be blamed?

Pope. It would have been nobler if we had not been parties in the quarrel. Our enemies observe that neither our censure nor our praise was always impartial.

Boileau. It might perhaps have been better if in some instances we had not praised or blamed so much. But in panegyric and satire moderation is insipid.

Pope. Moderation is a cold unpoetical virtue. Mere historical truth is better written in prose. And, therefore, I think you did judiciously when you threw into the fire your history of Louis le Grand, and trusted his fame to your poems.

Boileau. When those poems were published that monarch was the idol of the French nation. If you and I had not known, in our occasional compositions, how to speak to the passions, as well as to the sober reason of mankind, we should not have acquired that despotic authority in the empire of wit which made us so formidable to all the inferior tribe of poets in England and France. Besides, sharp satirists want great patrons.

Pope. All the praise which my friends received from me was unbought. In this, at least, I may boast a superiority over the pensioned Boileau.

Boileau. A pension in France was an honourable distinction. Had you been a Frenchman you would have ambitiously sought it; had I been an Englishman I should have proudly declined it. If our merit in other respects be not unequal, this difference will not set me much below you in the temple of virtue or of fame.

Pope. It is not for me to draw a comparison between our works. But, if I may believe the best critics who have talked to me on the subject, my "Rape of the Lock" is not inferior to your "Lutrin;" and my "Art of Criticism" may well be compared with your "Art of Poetry;" my "Ethic Epistles" are esteemed at least equal to yours; and my "Satires" much better.

Boileau. Hold, Mr. Pope. If there is really such a sympathy in our natures as you have supposed, there may be reason to fear that, if we go on in this manner comparing our works, we shall not part in good friendship.

Pope. No, no; the mild air of the Elysian Fields has mitigated my temper, as I presume it has yours. But, in truth, our reputations are nearly on a level. Our writings are admired, almost equally (as I hear) for energy and justness of thought. We both of us carried the beauty of our diction, and the harmony of our numbers, to the highest perfection that our languages would admit. Our poems were polished to the utmost degree of correctness, yet without losing their fire, or the agreeable appearance of freedom and ease. We borrowed much from the ancients, though you, I believe, more than I; but our imitations (to use an expression of your own) had still an original air.

Boileau. I will confess, sir (to show you that the Elysian climate has had its effects upon me), I will fairly confess, without the least ill humour, that in your "Eloisa to Abelard," your "Verses to the Memory of an Unfortunate Lady," and some others you wrote in your youth, there is more fire of poetry than in any of mine. You excelled in the pathetic, which I never approached. I will also allow that you hit the manner of Horace and the sly delicacy of his wit more exactly than I, or than any other man who has written since his time. Nor could I, nor did even Lucretius himself, make philosophy so poetical, and embellish it with such charms as you have given to that of Plato, or (to speak more properly) of some of his modern disciples, in your celebrated "Essay on Man."

Pope. What do you think of my "Homer?"

Boileau. Your "Homer" is the most spirited, the most poetical, the most elegant, and the most pleasing translation that ever was made of any ancient poem, though not so much in the manner of the original, or so exactly agreeable to the sense in all places, as might perhaps be desired. But when I consider the years you spent in this work, and how many excellent original poems you might, with less difficulty, have produced in that time, I can't but regret that your talents were thus employed. A great poet so tied down to a tedious translation is a Columbus chained to an oar. What new regions of fancy, full of treasures yet untouched, might you have explored, if you had been at liberty to have boldly expanded your sails, and steered your own course, under the conduct and direction of your own genius! But I am still more angry with you for your edition of Shakespeare. The office of an editor was below you, and your mind was unfit for the drudgery it requires. Would anybody think of employing a Raphael to clean an old picture?

Pope. The principal cause of my undertaking that task was zeal for the honour of Shakespeare; and, if you knew all his beauties as well as I, you would not wonder at this zeal. No other author had ever so copious, so bold, so creative an imagination, with so perfect a knowledge of the passions, the humours, and sentiments of mankind. He painted all characters, from kings down to peasants, with equal truth and equal force. If human nature were destroyed, and no monument were left of it except his works, other beings might know what man was from those writings.

Boileau. You say he painted all characters, from kings down to peasants, with equal truth and equal force. I can't deny that he did so; but I wish he had not jumbled those characters together in the composition of his pictures as he has frequently done.

Pope. The strange mixture of tragedy, comedy, and farce in the same play, nay, sometimes in the same scene, I acknowledge to be quite inexcusable. But this was the taste of the times when Shakespeare wrote.

Boileau. A great genius ought to guide, not servilely follow, the taste of his contemporaries.

Pope. Consider from how thick a darkness of barbarism the genius of Shakespeare broke forth! What were the English, and what, let me ask you, were the French dramatic performances, in the age when he nourished? The advances he made towards the highest perfection, both of tragedy and comedy, are amazing! In the principal points, in the power of exciting terror and pity, or raising laughter in an audience, none yet has excelled him, and very few have equalled.

Boileau. Do you think that he was equal in comedy to Moliere?

Pope. In comic force I do; but in the fine and delicate strokes of satire, and what is called genteel comedy, he was greatly inferior to that admirable writer. There is nothing in him to compare with the Misanthrope, the Ecole des Femmes, or Tartuffe.

Boileau. This, Mr. Pope, is a great deal for an Englishman to acknowledge. A veneration for Shakespeare seems to be a part of your national religion, and the only part in which even your men of sense are fanatics.

Pope. He who can read Shakespeare, and be cool enough for all the accuracy of sober criticism, has more of reason than taste.

Boileau. I join with you in admiring him as a prodigy of genius, though I find the most shocking absurdities in his plays, absurdities which no critic of my nation can pardon.

Pope. We will be satisfied with your feeling the excellence of his beauties. But you would admire him still more if you could see the chief characters in all his test tragedies represented by an actor who appeared on the stage a little before I left the world. He has shown the English nation more excellencies in Shakespeare than the quickest wits could discern, and has imprinted them on the heart with a livelier feeling than the most sensible natures had ever experienced without his help.

Boileau. The variety, spirit, and force of Mr. Garrick's action have been much praised to me by many of his countrymen, whose shades I converse with, and who agree in speaking of him as we do of Baron, our most natural and most admired actor. I have also heard of another, who has now quitted the stage, but who had filled, with great dignity, force, and elevation, some tragic parts, and excelled so much in the comic, that none ever has deserved a higher applause.

Pope. Mr. Quin was, indeed, a most perfect comedian. In the part of Falstaff particularly, wherein the utmost force of Shakespeare's humour appears, he attained to such perfection that he was not an actor; he was the man described by Shakespeare; he was Falstaff himself! When I saw him do it the pleasantry of the fat knight appeared to me so bewitching, all his vices were so mirthful, that I could not much wonder at his having seduced a young prince even to rob in his company.

Boileau. That character is not well understood by the French; they suppose it belongs, not to comedy, but to farce, whereas the English see in it the finest and highest strokes of wit and humour. Perhaps these different judgments may be accounted for in some measure by the diversity of manners in different countries. But don't you allow, Mr. Pope, that our writers, both of tragedy and comedy, are, upon the whole, more perfect masters of their art than yours? If you deny it, I will appeal to the Athenians, the only judges qualified to decide the dispute. I will refer it to Euripides, Sophocles, and Menander.

Pope. I am afraid of those judges, for I see them continually walking hand-in-hand, and engaged in the most friendly conversation with Corneille, Racine, and Moliere. Our dramatic writers seem, in general, not so fond of their company; they sometimes shove rudely by them, and give themselves airs of superiority. They slight their reprimands, and laugh at their precepts, in short, they will be tried by their country alone; and that judicature is partial.

Boileau. I will press this question no further. But let me ask you to which of our rival tragedians, Racine and Corneille, do you give the preference?

Pope. The sublimest plays of Corneille are, in my judgment, equalled by the Athalia of Racine, and the tender passions are certainly touched by that elegant and most pathetic writer with a much finer hand. I need not add that he is infinitely more correct than Corneille, and more harmonious and noble in his versification. Corneille formed himself entirely upon Lucan, but the master of Racine was Virgil. How much better a taste had the former than the latter in choosing his model!

Boileau. My friendship with Racine, and my partiality for his writings, make me hear with great pleasure the preference given to him above Corneille by so judicious a critic.

Pope. That he excelled his competitor in the particulars I have mentioned, can't, I think, be denied. But yet the spirit and the majesty of ancient Rome were never so well expressed as by Corneille. Nor has any other French dramatic writer, in the general character of his works, shown such a masculine strength and greatness of thought. Racine is the swan described by ancient poets, which rises to the clouds on downy wings and sings a sweet but a gentle and plaintive note. Corneille is the eagle, which soars to the skies on bold and sounding pinions, and fears not to perch on the sceptre of Jupiter, or to bear in his pounces the lightning of the god.

Boileau. I am glad to find, Mr. Pope, that in praising Corneille you run into poetry, which is not the language of sober criticism, though sometimes used by Longinus.

Pope. I caught the fire from the idea of Corneille.

Boileau. He has bright flashes, yet I think that in his thunder there is often more noise than fire. Don't you find him too declamatory, too turgid, too unnatural, even in his best tragedies?

Pope. I own I do; yet the greatness and elevation of his sentiments, and the nervous vigour of his sense, atone, in my opinion, for all his faults. But let me now, in my turn, desire your opinion of our epic poet, Milton.

Boileau. Longinus perhaps would prefer him to all other writers, for he surpasses even Homer in the sublime; but other critics who require variety, and agreeableness, and a correct regularity of thought and judgment in an epic poem, who can endure no absurdities, no extravagant fictions, would place him far below Virgil.

Pope. His genius was indeed so vast and sublime, that his poem seems beyond the limits of criticism, as his subject is beyond the limits of nature. The bright and excessive blaze of poetical fire, which shines in so many parts of the "Paradise Lost," will hardly permit the dazzled eye to see its faults.

Boileau. The taste of your countrymen is much changed since the days of Charles II., when Dryden was thought a greater poet than Milton!

Pope. The politics of Milton at that time brought his poetry into disgrace, for it is a rule with the English, they see no good in a man whose politics they dislike; but, as their notions of government are apt to change, men of parts whom they have slighted become their favourite authors, and others who have possessed their warmest admiration are in their turn undervalued. This revolution of favour was experienced by Dryden as well as Milton; he lived to see his writings, together with his politics, quite out of fashion. But even in the days of his highest prosperity, when the generality of the people admired his Almanzor, and thought his Indian Emperor the perfection of tragedy, the Duke of Buckingham and Lord Rochester, the two wittiest noblemen our country has produced, attacked his fame, and turned the rants of his heroes, the jargon of his spirits, and the absurdity of his plots into just ridicule.

Boileau. You have made him good amends by the praise you have given him in some of your writings.

Pope. I owed him that praise as my master in the art of versification, yet I subscribe to the censures which have been passed by other writers on many of his works. They are good critics, but he is still a great poet. You, sir, I am sure, must particularly admire him as an excellent satirist; his "Absalom and Achitophel" is a masterpiece in that way of writing, and his "Mac Flecno" is, I think, inferior to it in nothing but the meanness of the subject.

Boileau. Did not you take the model of your "Dunciad" from the latter of those very ingenious satires?

Pope. I did; but my work is more extensive than his, and my imagination has taken in it a greater scope.

Boileau. Some critics may doubt whether the length of your poem was so properly suited to the meanness of the subject as the brevity of his. Three cantos to expose a dunce crowned with laurel! I have not given above three lines to the author of the "Pucelle."

Pope. My intention was to expose, not one author alone, but all the dulness and false taste of the English nation in my times. Could such a design be contracted into a narrower compass?

Boileau. We will not dispute on this point, nor whether the hero of your "Dunciad" was really a dunce. But has not Dryden been accused of immorality and profaneness in some of his writings?

Pope. He has, with too much reason: and I am sorry to say that all our best comic writers after Shakespeare and Johnson, except Addison and Steele, are as liable as he to that heavy charge. Fletcher is shocking. Etheridge, Wycherley, Congreve, Vanbrugh, and Farquhar have painted the manners of the times in which they wrote with a masterly hand; but they are too often such manners that a virtuous man, and much more a virtuous woman, must be greatly offended at the representation.

Boileau. In this respect our stage is far preferable to yours. It is a school of morality. Vice is exposed to contempt and to hatred. No false colours are laid on to conceal its deformity, but those with which it paints itself are there taken off.

Pope. It is a wonderful thing that in France the comic Muse should be the gravest lady in the nation. Of late she is so grave, that one might almost mistake her for her sister Melpomene. Moliere made her indeed a good moral philosopher; but then she philosophised, like Democritus, with a merry, laughing face. Now she weeps over vice instead of showing it to mankind, as I think she generally ought to do, in ridiculous lights.

Boileau. Her business is more with folly than with vice, and when she attacks the latter, it should be rather with ridicule than invective. But sometimes she may be allowed to raise her voice, and change her usual smile into a frown of just indignation.

Pope. I like her best when she smiles. But did you never reprove your witty friend, La Fontaine, for the vicious levity that appears in many of his tales? He was as guilty of the crime of debauching the Muses as any of our comic poets.

Boileau. I own he was, and bewail the prostitution of his genius, as I should that of an innocent and beautiful country girl. He was all nature, all simplicity! yet in that simplicity there was a grace, and unaffected vivacity, with a justness of thought and easy elegance of expression that can hardly be found in any other writer. His manner is quite original, and peculiar to himself, though all the matter of his writings is borrowed from others.

Pope. In that manner he has been imitated by my friend Mr. Prior.

Boileau. He has, very successfully. Some of Prior's tales have the spirit of La Fontaine's with more judgment, but not, I think, with such an amiable and graceful simplicity.

Pope. Prior's harp had more strings than La Fontaine's. He was a fine poet in many different ways: La Fontaine but in one. And, though in some of his tales he imitated that author, his "Alma" was an original, and of singular beauty.

Boileau. There is a writer of heroic poetry, who lived before Milton, and whom some of your countrymen place in the highest class of your poets, though he is little known in France. I see him sometimes in company with Homer and Virgil, but oftener with Tasso, Ariosto, and Dante.

Pope. I understand you mean Spenser. There is a force and beauty in some of his images and descriptions, equal to any in those writers you have seen him converse with. But he had not the art of properly shading his pictures. He brings the minute and disagreeable parts too much into sight; and mingles too frequently vulgar and mean ideas with noble and sublime. Had he chosen a subject proper for epic poetry, he seems to have had a sufficient elevation and strength in his genius to make him a great epic poet: but the allegory, which is continued throughout the whole work, fatigues the mind, and cannot interest the heart so much as those poems, the chief actors in which are supposed to have really existed. The Syrens and Circe in the "Odyssey" are allegorical persons; but Ulysses, the hero of the poem, was a man renowned in Greece, which makes the account of his adventures affecting and delightful. To be now and then in Fairyland, among imaginary beings, is a pleasing variety, and helps to distinguish the poet from the orator or historian, but to be always there is irksome.

Boileau. Is not Spenser likewise blamable for confounding the Christian with the Pagan theology in some parts of his poem?

Pope. Yes; he had that fault in common with Dante, with Ariosto, and with Camoens.

Boileau. Who is the poet that arrived soon after you in Elysium, whom I saw Spenser lead in and present to Virgil, as the author of a poem resembling the "Georgics"? On his head was a garland of the several kinds of flowers that blow in each season, with evergreens intermixed.

Pope. Your description points out Thomson. He painted nature exactly, and with great strength of pencil. His imagination was rich, extensive, and sublime: his diction bold and glowing, but sometimes obscure and affected. Nor did he always know when to stop, or what to reject.

Boileau. I should suppose that he wrote tragedies upon the Greek model. For he is often admitted into the grove of Euripides.

Pope. He enjoys that distinction both as a tragedian and as a moralist. For not only in his plays, but all his other works, there is the purest morality, animated by piety, and rendered more touching by the fine and delicate sentiments of a most tender and benevolent heart.

Boileau. St. Evremond has brought me acquainted with Waller. I was surprised to find in his writings a politeness and gallantry which the French suppose to be appropriated only to theirs. His genius was a composition which is seldom to be met with, of the sublime and the agreeable. In his comparison between himself and Apollo, as the lover of Daphne, and in that between Amoret and Sacharissa, there is a finesse and delicacy of wit which the most elegant of our writers have never exceeded. Nor had Sarrazin or Voiture the art of praising more genteelly the ladies they admired. But his epistle to Cromwell, and his poem on the death of that extraordinary man, are written with a force and greatness of manner which give him a rank among the poets of the first class.

Pope. Mr. Waller was unquestionably a very fine writer. His Muse was as well qualified as the Graces themselves to dress out a Venus; and he could even adorn the brows of a conqueror with fragrant and beautiful wreaths. But he had some puerile and low thoughts, which unaccountably mixed with the elegant and the noble, like schoolboys or a mob admitted into a palace. There was also an intemperance and a luxuriancy in his wit which he did not enough restrain. He wrote little to the understanding, and less to the heart; but he frequently delights the imagination, and sometimes strikes it with flashes of the highest sublime. We had another poet of the age of Charles I., extremely admired by all his contemporaries, in whose works there is still more affectation of wit, a greater redundancy of imagination, a worse taste, and less judgment; but he touched the heart more, and had finer feelings than Waller. I mean Cowley.

Boileau. I have been often solicited to admire his writings by his learned friend, Dr. Spratt. He seems to me a great wit, and a very amiable man, but not a good poet.

Pope. The spirit of poetry is strong in some of his odes, but in the art of poetry he is always extremely deficient.

Boileau. I hear that of late his reputation is much lowered in the opinion of the English. Yet I cannot but think that, if a moderate portion of the superfluities of his wit were given by Apollo to some of their modern bards, who write commonplace morals in very smooth verse, without any absurdity, but without a single new thought, or one enlivening spark of imagination, it would be a great favour to them, and do them more service than all the rules laid down in my "Art of Poetry" and yours of "Criticism."

Pope. I am much of your mind. But I left in England some poets whom you, I know, will admire, not only for the harmony and correctness of style, but the spirit and genius you will find in their writings.

Boileau. France, too, has produced some very excellent writers since the time of my death. Of one particularly I hear wonders. Fame to him is as kind as if he had been dead a thousand years. She brings his praises to me from all parts of Europe. You know I speak of Voltaire.

Pope. I do; the English nation yields to none in admiration of his extensive genius. Other writers excel in some one particular branch of wit or science; but when the King of Prussia drew Voltaire from Paris to Berlin, he had a whole academy of belles lettres in him alone.

Boileau. That prince himself has such talents for poetry as no other monarch in any age or country has ever possessed. What an astonishing compass must there be in his mind, what an heroic tranquillity and firmness in his heart, that he can, in the evening, compose an ode or epistle in the most elegant verse, and the next morning fight a battle with the conduct of Caesar or Gustavus Adolphus!

Pope. I envy Voltaire so noble a subject both for his verse and his prose. But if that prince will write his own commentaries, he will want no historian. I hope that, in writing them, he will not restrain his pen, as Caesar has done, to a mere account of his wars, but let us see the politician, and the benignant protector of arts and sciences, as well as the warrior, in that picture of himself. Voltaire has shown us that the events of battles and sieges are not the most interesting parts of good history, but that all the improvements and embellishments of human society ought to be carefully and particularly recorded there.

Boileau. The progress of arts and knowledge, and the great changes that have happened in the manners of mankind, are objects far more worthy of a leader's attention than the revolutions of fortune. And it is chiefly to Voltaire that we owe this instructive species of history.

Pope. He has not only been the father of it among the moderns, but has carried it himself to its utmost perfection.

Boileau. Is he not too universal? Can any writer be exact who is so comprehensive?

Pope. A traveller round the world cannot inspect every region with such an accurate care as exactly to describe each single part. If the outlines are well marked, and the observations on the principal points are judicious, it is all that can be required.

Boileau. I would, however, advise and exhort the French and English youth to take a fuller survey of some particular provinces, and to remember that although, in travels of this sort, a lively imagination is a very agreeable companion, it is not the best guide. To speak without a metaphor, the study of history, both sacred and profane, requires a critical and laborious investigation. The composer of a set of lively and witty remarks on facts ill-examined, or incorrectly delivered, is not an historian.

Pope. We cannot, I think, deny that name to the author of the "Life of Charles XII., King of Sweden."

Boileau. No, certainly. I esteem it the very best history that this age has produced. As full of spirit as the hero whose actions it relates, it is nevertheless most exact in all matters of importance. The style of it is elegant, perspicuous, unaffected; the disposition and method are excellent; the judgments given by the writer acute and just.

Pope. Are you not pleased with that philosophical freedom of thought which discovers itself in all the works of Voltaire, but more particularly in those of an historical nature?

Boileau. If it were properly regulated, I should reckon it among their highest perfections. Superstition, and bigotry, and party spirit are as great enemies to the truth and candour of history as malice or adulation. To think freely is therefore a most necessary quality in a perfect historian. But all liberty has its bounds, which, in some of his writings, Voltaire, I fear, has not observed. Would to Heaven he would reflect, while it is yet in his power to correct what is faulty, that all his works will outlive him; that many nations will read them; and that the judgment pronounced here upon the writer himself will be according to the scope and tendency of them, and to the extent of their good or evil effects on the great society of mankind.

Pope. It would be well for all Europe if some other wits of your country, who give the tone to this age in all polite literature, had the same serious thoughts you recommend to Voltaire. Witty writings, when directed to serve the good ends of virtue and religion, are like the lights hung out in a pharos, to guide the mariners safe through dangerous seas; but the brightness of those that are impious or immoral shines only to betray and lead men to destruction.

Boileau. Has England been free from all seductions of this nature?

Pope. No. But the French have the art of rendering vice and impiety more agreeable than the English.

Boileau. I am not very proud of this superiority in the talents of my countrymen. But as I am told that the good sense of the English is now admired in France, I hope it will soon convince both nations that true wisdom is virtue, and true virtue is religion.

Pope. I think it also to be wished that a taste for the frivolous may not continue too prevalent among the French. There is a great difference between gathering flowers at the foot of Parnassus and ascending the arduous heights of the mountain. The palms and laurels grow there, and if any of your countrymen aspire to gain them, they must no longer enervate all the vigour of their minds by this habit of trifling. I would have them be perpetual competitors with the English in manly wit and substantial learning. But let the competition be friendly. There is nothing which so contracts and debases the mind as national envy. True wit, like true virtue, naturally loves its own image in whatever place it is found.

DIALOGUE XV. OCTAVIA – PORTIA - ARRIA.

Portia. How has it happened, Octavia, that Arria and I, who have a higher rank than you in the Temple of Fame, should have a lower here in Elysium? We are told that the virtues you exerted as a wife were greater than ours. Be so good as to explain to us what were those virtues. It is the privilege of this place that one can bear superiority without mortification. The jealousy of precedence died with the rest of our mortal frailties. Tell us, then, your own story. We will sit down under the shade of this myrtle grove and listen to it with pleasure.

Octavia. Noble ladies, the glory of our sex and of Rome, I will not refuse to comply with your desire, though it recalls to my mind some scenes my heart would wish to forget. There can be only one reason why Minos should have given to my conjugal virtues a preference above yours, which is that the trial assigned to them was harder.

Arria. How, madam! harder than to die for your husband! We died for ours. Octavia. You did for husbands who loved yon, and were the most virtuous men of the ages they lived in, who trusted you with their lives, their fame, their honour. To outlive such husbands is, in my judgment, a harder effort of virtue than to die for them or with them. But Mark Antony, to whom my brother Octavius, for reasons of state, gave my hand, was indifferent to me, and loved another. Yet he has told me himself I was handsomer than his mistress Cleopatra. Younger I certainly was, and to men that is generally a charm sufficient to turn the scale in one's favour. I had been loved by Marcellus. Antony said he loved me when he pledged to me his faith. Perhaps he did for a time; a new handsome woman might, from his natural inconstancy, make him forget an old attachment. He was but too amiable. His very vices had charms beyond other men's virtues. Such vivacity! such fire! such a towering pride! He seemed made by nature to command, to govern the world; to govern it with such ease that the business of it did not rob him of an hour of pleasure. Nevertheless, while his inclination for me continued, this haughty lord of mankind who could hardly bring his high spirit to treat my brother, his partner in empire, with the necessary respect, was to me as submissive, as obedient to every wish of my heart, as the humblest lover that ever sighed in the vales of Arcadia. Thus he seduced my affection from the manes of Marcellus and fixed it on himself. He fixed it, ladies (I own it with some confusion), more fondly than it had ever been fixed on Marcellus. And when he had done so he scorned me, he forsook me, he returned to Cleopatra. Think who I was, the sister of Caesar, sacrificed to a vile Egyptian queen, the harlot of Julius, the disgrace of her sex! Every outrage was added that could incense me still more. He gave her at sundry times, as public marks of his love, many provinces of the Empire of Rome in the East. He read her love-letters openly in his tribunal itself, even while he was hearing and judging the causes of kings. Nay, he left his tribunal, and one of the best Roman orators pleading before him, to follow her litter, in which she happened to be passing by at that time. But, what was more grievous to me than all these demonstrations of his extravagant passion for that infamous woman, he had the assurance, in a letter to my brother, to call her his wife. Which of you, ladies, could have patiently borne this treatment?

Arria. Not I, madam, in truth. Had I been in your place, the dagger with which I pierced my own bosom to show my dear Paetus how easy it was to die, that dagger should I have plunged into Antony's heart, if piety to the gods and a due respect to the purity of my own soul had not stopped my hand. But I verily believe I should have killed myself; not, as I did, out of affection to my husband, but out of shame and indignation at the wrongs I endured.

Portia. I must own, Octavia, that to bear such usage was harder to a woman than to swallow fire.

Octavia. Yet I did bear it, madam, without even a complaint which could hurt or offend my husband. Nay, more, at his return from his Parthian expedition, which his impatience to bear a long absence from Cleopatra had made unfortunate and inglorious, I went to meet him in Syria, and carried with me rich presents of clothes and money for his troops, a great number of horses, and two thousand chosen soldiers, equipped and armed like my brother's Praetorian bands. He sent to stop me at Athens because his mistress was then with him. I obeyed his orders; but I wrote to him, by one of his most faithful friends, a letter full of resignation, and such a tenderness for him as I imagined might have power to touch his heart. My envoy served me so well, he set my fidelity in so fair a light, and gave such reasons to Antony why he ought to see and receive me with kindness, that Cleopatra was alarmed. All her arts were employed to prevent him from seeing me, and to draw him again into Egypt. Those arts prevailed. He sent me back into Italy, and gave himself up more absolutely than ever to the witchcraft of that Circe. He added Africa to the States he had bestowed on her before, and declared Caesario, her spurious son by Julius Caesar, heir to all her dominions, except Phoenicia and Cilicia, which with the Upper Syria he gave to Ptolemy, his second son by her; and at the same time declared his eldest son by her, whom he had espoused to the Princess of Media, heir to that kingdom and King of Armenia; nay, and of the whole Parthian Empire which he meant to conquer for him. The children I had brought him he entirely neglected as if they had been bastards. I wept. I lamented the wretched captivity he was in; but I never reproached him. My brother, exasperated at so many indignities, commanded me to quit the house of my husband at Rome and come into his. I refused to obey him. I remained in Antony's house; I persisted to take care of his children by Fulvia, the same tender care as of my own. I gave my protection to all his friends at Rome. I implored my brother not to make my jealousy or my wrongs the cause of a civil war. But the injuries done to Rome by Antony's conduct could not possibly be forgiven. When he found he should draw the Roman arms on himself, he sent orders to me to leave his house. I did so, but carried with me all his children by Fulvia, except Antyllus, the eldest, who was then with him in Egypt. After his death and Cleopatra's, I took her children by him, and bred them up with my own.

Arria. Is it possible, madam? the children of Cleopatra?

Octavia. Yes, the children of my rival. I married her daughter to Juba, King of Mauritania, the most accomplished and the handsomest prince in the world.

Arria. Tell me, Octavia, did not your pride and resentment entirely cure you of your passion for Antony, as soon as you saw him go back to Cleopatra? And was not your whole conduct afterwards the effect of cool reason, undisturbed by the agitations of jealous and tortured love?

Octavia. You probe my heart very deeply. That I had some help from resentment and the natural pride of my sex, I will not deny. But I was not become indifferent to my husband. I loved the Antony who had been my lover, more than I was angry with the Antony who forsook me and loved another woman. Had he left Cleopatra and returned to me again with all his former affection, I really believe I should have loved him as well as before.

Arria. If the merit of a wife is to be measured by her sufferings, your heart was unquestionably the most perfect model of conjugal virtue. The wound I gave mine was but a scratch in comparison to many you felt. Yet I don't know whether it would be any benefit to the world that there should be in it many Octavias. Too good subjects are apt to make bad kings.

Portia. True, Arria; the wives of Brutus and Cecinna Paetus may be allowed to have spirits a little rebellious. Octavia was educated in the Court of her brother. Subjection and patience were much better taught there than in our houses, where the Roman liberty made its last abode. And though I will not dispute the judgment of Minos, I can't help thinking that the affection of a wife to her husband is more or less respectable in proportion to the character of that husband. If I could have had for Antony the same friendship as I had for Brutus, I should have despised myself.

Octavia. My fondness for Antony was ill-placed; but my perseverance in the performance of all the duties of a wife, notwithstanding his ill-usage, a perseverance made more difficult by the very excess of my love, appeared to Minos the highest and most meritorious effort of female resolution against the seductions of the most dangerous enemy to our virtue, offended pride.

DIALOGUE XVI. LOUISE DE COLIGNI, PRINCESS OF ORANGE - FRANCES WALSINGHAM, COUNTESS OF ESSEX AND OF CLANRICARDE; BEFORE, LADY SIDNEY.

Princess of Orange. Our destinies, madam, had a great and surprising conformity. I was the daughter of Admiral Coligni, you of Secretary Walsingham, two persons who were the most consummate statesmen and ablest supports of the Protestant religion in France, and in England. I was married to Teligni, the finest gentleman of our party, the most admired for his valour, his virtue, and his learning: you to Sir Philip Sidney, who enjoyed the same pre-eminence among the English. Both these husbands were cut off, in the flower of youth and of glory, by violent deaths, and we both married again with still greater men; I with William Prince of Orange, the founder of the Dutch Commonwealth; you with Devereux Earl of Essex, the favourite of Elizabeth and of the whole English nation. But, alas! to complete the resemblance of our fates, we both saw those second husbands, who had raised us so high, destroyed in the full meridian of their glory and greatness: mine by the pistol of an assassin; yours still more unhappily, by the axe, as a traitor.

Countess of Clanricarde. There was indeed in some principal events of our lives the conformity you observe. But your destiny, though it raised you higher than me, was more unhappy than mine. For my father lived honourably, and died in peace: yours was assassinated in his old age. How, madam, did you support or recover your spirits under so rainy misfortunes?

Princess of Orange. The Prince of Orange left an infant son to my care. The educating of him to be worthy of so illustrious a father, to be the heir of his virtue as well as of his greatness, and the affairs of the commonwealth, in which I interested myself for his sake, so filled my mind, that they in some measure took from me the sense of my grief, which nothing but such a great and important scene of business, such a necessary talk of private and public duty, could have ever relieved. But let me inquire in my turn, how did your heart find a balm to alleviate the anguish of the wounds it had suffered? What employed your widowed hours after the death of your Essex?

Countess of Clanricarde. Madam, I did not long continue a widow: I married again.

Princess of Orange. Married again! With what prince, what king did you marry? The widow of Sir Philip Sidney and of my Lord Essex could not descend from them to a subject of less illustrious fame; and where could you find one that was comparable to either?

Countess of Clanricarde. I did not seek for one, madam: the heroism of the former, and the ambition of the latter, had made me very unhappy. I desired a quiet life and the joys of wedded love, with an agreeable, virtuous, well-born, unambitious, unenterprising husband. All this I found in the Earl of Clanricarde: and believe me, madam, I enjoyed more solid felicity in Ireland with him, than I ever had possessed with my two former husbands, in the pride of their glory, when England and all Europe resounded with their praise.

Princess of Orange. Can it be possible that the daughter of Walsingham, and the wife of Sidney and Essex, should have sentiments so inferior to the minds from which she sprang, and to which she was matched? Believe me, madam, there was no hour of the many years I lived after the death of the

Prince of Orange, in which I would have exchanged the pride and joy I continually had in hearing his praise, and seeing the monuments of his glory in the free commonwealth his wisdom had founded, for any other delights the world could give. The cares that I shared with him, while he remained upon earth, were a happiness to my mind, because they exalted its powers. The remembrance of them was dear to me after I had lost him. I thought his great soul, though removed to a higher sphere, would look down upon mine with some tenderness of affection, as its fellow-labourer in the heroic and divine work of delivering and freeing his country. But to be divorced from that soul! to be no longer his wife! to be the comfort of an inferior, inglorious husband! I had much rather have died a thousand deaths, than that my heart should one moment have conceived such a thought.

Countess of Clanricarde. Your Highness must not judge of all hearts by your own. The ruling passion of that was apparently ambition. My inclinations were not so noble as yours, but better suited, perhaps, to the nature of woman. I loved Sir Philip Sidney, I loved the Earl of Essex, rather as amiable men than as heroes and statesmen. They were so taken up with their wars and state-affairs, that my tenderness for them was too often neglected. The Earl of Clanricarde was constantly and wholly mine. He was brave, but had not that spirit of chivalry with which Sir Philip Sidney was absolutely possessed. He had, in a high degree, the esteem of Elizabeth, but did not aspire to her love; nor did he wish to be the rival of Carr or of Villiers in the affection of James. Such, madam, was the man on whom my last choice bestowed my hand, and whose kindness compensated for all my misfortunes. Providence has assigned to different tempers different comforts. To you it gave the education of a prince, the government of a state, the pride of being called the wife of a hero; to me a good-living husband, quiet, opulence, nobility, and a fair reputation, though not in a degree so exalted as yours. If our whole sex were to choose between your consolations and mine, your Highness, I think, would find very few of your taste. But I respect the sublimity of your ideas. Now that we have no bodies they appear less unnatural than I should have thought them in the other world.

Princess of Orange. Adieu, madam. Our souls are of a different order, and were not made to sympathise or converse with each other.

DIALOGUE XVII. MARCUS BRUTUS - POMPONIUS ATTICUS.

Brutus. Well, Atticus, I find that, notwithstanding your friendship for Cicero and for me, you survived us both many years, with the same cheerful spirit you had always possessed, and, by prudently wedding your daughter to Agrippa, secured the favour of Octavius Caesar, and even contracted a close alliance with him by your granddaughter's marriage with Tiberius Nero.

Atticus. You know, Brutus, my philosophy was the Epicurean. I loved my friends, and I served them in their wants and distresses with great generosity; but I did not think myself obliged to die when they died, or not to make others as occasions should offer.

Brutus. You did, I acknowledge, serve your friends, as far as you could, without bringing yourself, on their account, into any great danger or disturbance of mind: but that you loved them I much doubt. If you loved Cicero, how could you love Antony? If you loved me, how could you love Octavius? If you loved Octavius, how could you avoid taking part against Antony in their last civil war? Affection cannot be so strangely divided, and with so much equality, among men of such opposite characters, and who were such irreconcilable enemies to each other.

Atticus. From my earliest youth I possessed the singular talent of ingratiating myself with the heads of different parties, and yet not engaging with any of them so far as to disturb my own quiet. My family was connected with the Marian party; and, though I retired to Athens that I might not be unwillingly involved in the troubles which that turbulent faction had begun to excite, yet when young Marius was declared an enemy by the Senate, I sent him a sum of money to support him in his exile. Nor did this hinder me from making my court so well to Sylla, upon his coming to Athens, that I obtained from him the highest marks of his favour. Nevertheless, when he pressed me to go with him to Rome, I declined it, being as unwilling to fight for him against the Marian party, as for them against him. He admired my conduct; and at his departure from Athens, ordered all the presents made to him during his abode in that city to be carried to me. I remind you of this only to show that moderation in all contentions of this kind had been always my principle; and that in the instances you mentioned I did not act from any levity or inconstancy in my nature, but from a regular consistent plan of conduct, which my reason convinced me was the wisest I could follow.

Brutus. I remember indeed that you observed the same neutrality between Pompey and Julius Caesar.

Atticus. I did so, and that I might be able to do it with dignity, and without the reproach of ingratitude, I never would accept any office or honour from either of those great men; nor from Cicero, though my sister had married his brother; nor from you, Marcus Brutus, whose friendship I thought the greatest honour of my life.

Brutus. Are there no obligations to a good heart, Pomponius, but honours and offices? Or could you, by refusing to encumber yourself with these, dissolve all other ties? But, setting aside any considerations of private affection or esteem, how was you able to reconcile your conduct with that which is the ruling principle in the heart of every virtuous man, and more especially a virtuous Roman, the love of the public?

Atticus. The times I lived in were so bad, and the conflict of parties had so little to do in reality with the love of the public, that I thought my virtue much safer and purer by avoiding than mixing in the fray.

Brutus. Possibly, in the dispute between Marius and Sylla, and even in that between Pompey and Caesar, a virtuous man might see so much to blame on both sides, and so much to fear, whichever faction should overcome the other, as to be justified in not engaging with either. But let me say, without vanity, in the war which I waged against Antony and Octavius you could have nothing to blame, for I know you approved the principle upon which I killed Julius Caesar. Nor had you anything to fear if our arms had succeeded, for you know that my intentions were upright and pure; nor was it doubtful that Cassius was as much determined as I to restore the Republic. How could you, then, with any sense of virtue in your heart, maintain an indifference and neutrality between the deliverers and the tyrants of your country?

Atticus. My answer to this will necessarily require explanations, which my respect to the manes of Brutus makes me wish to avoid.

Brutus. In the other world I loved truth, and was desirous that all might speak it with freedom; but here even the tender ears of a tyrant are compelled to endure it. If I committed any faults, or erred in my judgment, the calamities I have suffered are a punishment for it. Tell me then, truly, and without fear of offending, what you think were my failings.

Atticus. You said that the principle upon which you killed Julius Caesar had my approbation. This I do not deny; but did I ever declare, or give you reason to believe, that I thought it a prudent or well-timed act? I had quite other thoughts. Nothing ever seemed to me worse judged or worse timed; and these, Brutus, were my reasons. Caesar was just setting out to make war on the Parthians. This was an enterprise of no little difficulty and no little danger; but his unbounded ambition, and that restless spirit which never would suffer him to take any repose, did not intend to stop there. You know very well (for he hid nothing from you) that he had formed a vast plan of marching, after he had conquered the whole Parthian Empire, along the coast of the Caspian Sea and the sides of Mount Caucasus into Scythia, in order to subdue all the countries that border on Germany, and Germany itself; from whence he proposed to return to Rome by Gaul. Consider now, I beseech you, how much time the execution of this project required. In some of his battles with so many fierce and warlike nations, the bravest of all the barbarians, he might have been slain; but, if he had not, disease, or age itself, might have ended his life before he could have completed such an immense undertaking. He was, when you killed him, in his fifty-sixth year, and of an infirm constitution. Except his bastard by Cleopatra, he had no son; nor was his power so absolute or so quietly settled that he could have a thought of bequeathing the Empire, like a private inheritance, to his sister's grandson, Octavius. While he was absent there was no reason to fear any violence or maladministration in Italy or in Rome. Cicero would have had the chief authority in the Senate. The praetorship of the city had been conferred upon you by the favour of Caesar, and your known credit with him, added to the high reputation of your virtues and abilities, gave you a weight in all business which none of his party left behind him in Italy would have been able to oppose. What a fair prospect was here of good order, peace, and liberty at home, while abroad the Roman name would have been rendered more glorious, the disgrace of Crassus revenged, and the Empire extended beyond the utmost ambition of our forefathers by the greatest general that ever led the armies of Rome, or, perhaps, of any other nation! What did it signify whether in Asia, and among the barbarians, that general bore the name of King or Dictator? Nothing could be more puerile in you and your friends than to start so much at the proposition of his taking that name in Italy itself, when you had suffered him to enjoy all the power of royalty, and much more than any King of Rome had possessed from Romulus down to Tarquin.

Brutus. We considered that name as the last insult offered to our liberty and our laws; it was an ensign of tyranny, hung out with a vain and arrogant purpose of rendering the servitude of Rome more apparent. We, therefore, determined to punish the tyrant, and restore our country to freedom.

Atticus. You punished the tyrant, but you did not restore your country to freedom. By sparing Antony, against the opinion of Cassius, you suffered the tyranny to remain. He was Consul, and, from the moment that Caesar was dead, the chief power of the State was in his hands. The soldiers adored him for his liberality, valour, and military frankness. His eloquence was more persuasive from appearing unstudied. The nobility of his house, which descended from Hercules, would naturally inflame his heart with ambition. The whole course of his life had evidently shown that his thoughts were high and aspiring, and that he had little respect for the liberty of his country. He had been the second man in Caesar's party; by saving him you gave a new head to that party, which could no longer subsist without your ruin. Many who would have wished the restoration of liberty, if Caesar had died a natural death, were so incensed at his murder that, merely for the sake of punishing that, they were willing to confer all power upon Antony and make him absolute master of the Republic. This was particularly true with respect to the veterans who had served under Caesar, and he saw it so plainly that he presently availed himself of their dispositions. You and Cassius were obliged to fly out of Italy, and Cicero, who was unwilling to take the same part, could find no expedient to save himself and the Senate but the wretched one of supporting and raising very high another Caesar, the adopted son and heir of him you had slain, to oppose Antony and to divide the Caesarean party. But even while he did this he perpetually offended that party and made them his enemies by harangues in the Senate, which breathed the very spirit of the old Pompeian faction, and made him appear to Octavius and all the friends of the dead Dictator no less guilty of his death than those who had killed him. What could this end in but that which you and your friends had most to fear, a reunion of the whole Caesarean party and of their principal leaders, however discordant the one with the other, to destroy the Pompeians? For my own part, I foresaw it long before the event, and therefore kept myself wholly clear of those proceedings. You think I ought to have joined you and Cassius at Philippi, because I knew your good intentions, and that, if you succeeded, you designed to restore the commonwealth. I am persuaded you did both agree in that point, but you differed in so many others, there was such a dissimilitude in your tempers and characters, that the union between you could not have lasted long, and your dissension would have had most fatal effects with regard both to the settlement and to the administration of the Republic. Besides, the whole mass of it was in such a fermentation, and so corrupted, that I am convinced new disorders would soon have arisen. If you had applied gentle remedies, to which your nature inclined, those remedies would have failed; if Cassius had induced you to act with severity, your government would have been stigmatised with the name of a tyranny more detestable than that against which you conspired, and Caesar's clemency would have been the perpetual topic of every factious oration to the people, and of every seditious discourse to the soldiers. Thus you would have soon been plunged in the miseries of another civil war, or perhaps assassinated in the Senate, as Julius was by you. Nothing could give the Roman Empire a lasting tranquillity but such a prudent plan of a mitigated imperial power as was afterwards formed by Octavius, when he had ably and happily delivered himself from all opposition and partnership in the government. Those quiet times I lived to see, and I must say they were the best I ever had seen, far better than those under the turbulent aristocracy for which you contended. And let me boast a little of my own prudence, which, through so many storms, could steer me safe into that port. Had it only given me safety, without reputation, I should not think that I ought to value myself upon it. But in all these revolutions my honour remained as unimpaired as my fortune. I so conducted myself that I lost no esteem in being Antony's friend after having been Cicero's, or in my alliance with Agrippa and Augustus Caesar after my friendship with you. Nor did either Caesar or Antony blame my inaction in the quarrels between them; but, on the contrary, they both seemed to respect me the more for the neutrality I observed. My obligations to the one and alliance with the other made it improper for me to act against either, and my constant tenor of life had procured me an exemption from all civil wars by a kind of prescription.

Brutus. If man were born to no higher purpose than to wear out a long life in ease and prosperity, with the general esteem of the world, your wisdom was evidently as much superior to mine as my life was shorter and more unhappy than yours. Nay, I verily believe it exceeded the prudence of any other man that ever existed, considering in what difficult circumstances you were placed, and with how many violent shocks and sudden changes of fortune you were obliged to contend. But here the most virtuous and public-spirited conduct is found to have been the most prudent. The motives of our actions, not the success, give us here renown. And could I return to that life from whence I am escaped, I would not change my character to imitate yours; I would again be Brutus rather than Atticus. Even without the sweet hope of an eternal reward in a more perfect state, which is the strongest and most immovable support to the good under every misfortune, I swear by the gods I would not give up the noble feelings of my heart, that elevation of mind which accompanies active and suffering virtue, for your seventy-seven years of constant tranquillity, with all the praise you obtained from the learned men whom you patronised or the great men whom you courted.

DIALOGUE XVIII. WILLIAM III., KING OF ENGLAND - JOHN DE WITT, PENSIONER, OF HOLLAND.

William. Though I had no cause to love you, yet, believe me, I sincerely lament your fate. Who could have thought that De Witt, the most popular Minister that ever served a commonwealth, should fall a sacrifice to popular fury! Such admirable talents, such virtues as you were endowed with, so clear, so cool, so comprehensive a head, a heart so untainted with any kind of vice, despising money, despising pleasure, despising the vain ostentation of greatness, such application to business, such ability in it, such courage, such firmness, and so perfect a knowledge of the nation you governed, seemed to assure you of a fixed and stable support in the public affection. But nothing can be durable that depends on the passions of the people.

De Witt. It is very generous in your Majesty, not only to compassionate the fate of a man whose political principles made him an enemy to your greatness, but to ascribe it to the caprice and inconstancy of the people, as if there had been nothing very blamable in his conduct. I feel the magnanimity of this discourse from your Majesty, and it confirms what I have heard of all your behaviour after my death. But I must frankly confess that, although the rage of the populace was carried much too far when they tore me and my unfortunate brother to pieces, yet I certainly had deserved to lose their affection by relying too much on the uncertain and dangerous friendship of France, and by weakening the military strength of the State, to serve little purposes of my own power, and secure to myself the interested affection of the burgomasters or others who had credit and weight in the faction the favour of which I courted. This had almost subjected my country to France, if you, great prince, had not been set at the head of the falling Republic, and had not exerted such extraordinary virtues and abilities to raise and support it, as surpassed even the heroism and prudence of William, our first Stadtholder, and equalled yon to the most illustrious patriots of Greece or Rome.

William. This praise from your mouth is glorious to me indeed! What can so much exalt the character of a prince as to have his actions approved by a zealous Republican and the enemy of his house?

De Witt. If I did not approve them I should show myself the enemy of the Republic. You never sought to tyrannise over it; you loved, you defended, you preserved its freedom. Thebes was not more indebted to Epaminondas or Pelopidas for its independence and glory than the United Provinces were to you. How wonderful was it to see a youth, who had scarce attained to the twenty-second year of his age, whose spirit had been depressed and kept down by a jealous and hostile faction, rising at once to the conduct of a most arduous and perilous war, stopping an enemy victorious, triumphant, who had penetrated into the heart of his country, driving him back and recovering from him all he had conquered: to see this done with an army in which a little before there was neither discipline, courage, nor sense of honour! Ancient history has no exploit superior to it; and it will ennoble the modern whenever a Livy or a Plutarch shall arise to do justice to it, and set the hero who performed it in a true light.

William. Say, rather, when time shall have worn out that malignity and rancour of party which in free States is so apt to oppose itself to the sentiments of gratitude and esteem for their servants and benefactors.

De Witt. How magnanimous was your reply, how much in the spirit of true ancient virtue, when being asked, in the greatest extremity of our danger, "How you intended to live after Holland was lost?" you said, "You would live on the lands you had left in Germany, and had rather pass your life in hunting there than sell your country or liberty to France at any rate!" How nobly did you think when, being offered your patrimonial lordships and lands in the county of Burgundy, or the full value of them from France, by the mediation of England in the treaty of peace, your answer was, "That to gain one good town more for the Spaniards in Flanders you would be content to lose them all!" No wonder, after this, that you were able to combine all Europe in a league against the power of France; that you were the centre of union, and the directing soul of that wise, that generous confederacy formed by your labours; that you could steadily support and keep it together, in spite of repeated misfortunes; that even after defeats you were as formidable to Louis as other generals after victories; and that in the end you became the deliverer of Europe, as you had before been of Holland.

William. I had, in truth, no other object, no other passion at heart throughout my whole life but to maintain the independence and freedom of Europe against the ambition of France. It was this desire which formed the whole plan of my policy, which animated all my counsels, both as Prince of Orange and King of England.

De Witt. This desire was the most noble (I speak it with shame) that could warm the heart of a prince whose ancestors had opposed and in a great measure destroyed the power of Spain when that nation aspired to the monarchy of Europe. France, sir, in your days had an equal ambition and more strength to support her vast designs than Spain under the government of Philip II. That ambition you restrained, that strength you resisted. I, alas! was seduced by her perfidious Court, and by the necessity of affairs in that system of policy which I had adopted, to ask her assistance, to rely on her favour, and to make the commonwealth, whose counsels I directed, subservient to her greatness. Permit me, sir, to explain to you the motives of my conduct. If all the Princes of Orange had acted like you, I should never have been the enemy of your house. But Prince Maurice of Nassau desired to oppress the liberty of that State which his virtuous father had freed at the expense of his life, and which he himself had defended against the arms of the House of Austria with the highest reputation of military abilities. Under a pretence of religion (the most execrable cover of a wicked design) he put to death, as a criminal, that upright Minister, Barneveldt, his father's best friend, because, he refused to concur with him in treason against the State. He likewise imprisoned several other good men and lovers of their country, confiscated their estates, and ruined their families. Yet, after he had done these cruel acts of injustice with a view to make himself sovereign of the Dutch Commonwealth, he found they had drawn such a general odium upon him that, not daring to accomplish his iniquitous purpose, he stopped short of the tyranny to which he had sacrificed his honour and virtue; a disappointment so mortifying and so painful to his mind that it probably hastened his death.

William. Would to Heaven he had died before the meeting of that infamous Synod of Dort, by which he not only dishonoured himself and his family, but the Protestant religion itself! Forgive this interruption, my grief forced me to it, I desire you to proceed.

De Witt. The brother of Maurice, Prince Henry, who succeeded to his dignities in the Republic, acted with more moderation. But the son of that good prince, your Majesty's father (I am sorry to speak what I know you hear with pain), resumed, in the pride and fire of his youth, the ambitious designs of his uncle. He failed in his undertaking, and soon afterwards died, but left in the hearts of the whole Republican party an incurable jealousy and dread of his family. Full of these prejudices, and zealous for liberty, I thought it my duty as Pensionary of Holland to prevent for ever, if I could, your restoration to the power your ancestors had enjoyed, which I sincerely believed would be inconsistent with the safety and freedom of my country.

William. Let me stop you a moment here. When my great-grandfather formed the plan of the Dutch Commonwealth, he made the power of a Stadtholder one of the principal springs in his system of government. How could you imagine that it would ever go well when deprived of this spring, so necessary to adjust and balance its motions? A constitution originally formed with no mixture of regal power may long be maintained in all its vigour and energy without such a power; but if any degree of monarchy was mixed from the beginning in the principles of it, the forcing that out must necessarily disorder and weaken the whole fabric. This was particularly the case in our Republic. The negative voice of every small town in the provincial States, the tedious slowness of our forms and deliberations, the facility with which foreign Ministers may seduce or purchase the opinions of so many persons as have a right to concur in all our resolutions, make it impossible for the Government, even in the quietest times, to be well carried on without the authority and influence of a Stadtholder, which are the only remedy our constitution has provided for those evils.

De Witt. I acknowledge they are; but I and my party thought no evil so great as that remedy, and therefore we sought for other more pleasing resources. One of these, upon which we most confidently depended, was the friendship of France. I flattered myself that the interest of the French would secure to me their favour, as your relation to the Crown of England might naturally raise in them a jealousy of your power. I hoped they would encourage the trade and commerce of the Dutch in opposition to the English, the ancient enemies of their Crown, and let us enjoy all the benefits of a perpetual peace, unless we made war upon England, or England upon us, in either of which cases it was reasonable to presume we should have their assistance. The French Minister at the Hague, who served his Court but too well, so confirmed me in these notions, that I had no apprehensions of the mine which was forming under my feet.

William. You found your authority strengthened by a plan so agreeable to your party, and this contributed more to deceive your sagacity than all the art of D'Estrades.

De Witt. My policy seemed to me entirely suitable to the lasting security of my own power, of the liberty of my country, and of its maritime greatness; for I made it my care to keep up a very powerful navy, well commanded and officered, for the defence of all these against the English; but, as I feared nothing from France, or any Power on the Continent, I neglected the army, or rather I destroyed it, by enervating all its strength, by disbanding old troops and veteran officers attached to the House of Orange, and putting in their place a trading militia, commanded by officers who had neither experience nor courage, and who owed their promotions to no other merit but their relation to or interest with some leading men in the several oligarchies of which the Government in all the Dutch towns is composed. Nevertheless, on the invasion of Flanders by the French, I was forced to depart from my close connection with France, and to concur with England and Sweden in the Triple Alliance, which Sir William Temple proposed, in order to check her ambition; but as I entered into that measure from necessity, not from choice, I did not pursue it. I neglected to improve our union with England, or to secure that with Sweden; I avoided any conjunction of counsels with Spain; I formed no alliance with the Emperor or the Germans; I corrupted our army more and more; till a sudden, unnatural confederacy, struck up, against all the maxims of policy, by the Court of England with France, for the conquest of the Seven Provinces, brought these at once to the very brink of destruction, and made me a victim to the fury of a populace too justly provoked.

William. I must say that your plan was in reality nothing more than to procure for the Dutch a licence to trade under the good pleasure and gracious protection of France. But any State that so entirely depends on another is only a province, and its liberty is a servitude graced with a sweet but empty name. You should have reflected that to a monarch so ambitious and so vain as Louis le Grand the idea of a conquest which seemed almost certain, and the desire of humbling a haughty Republic, were temptations irresistible. His bigotry likewise would concur in recommending to him an enterprise which he might think would put heresy under his feet. And if you knew either the character of Charles II. or the principles of his government, you ought not to have supposed his union with France for the ruin of Holland an impossible or even improbable event. It is hardly excusable in a statesman to be greatly surprised that the inclinations of princes should prevail upon them to act, in many particulars, without any regard to the political maxims and interests of their kingdoms.

De Witt. I am ashamed of my error; but the chief cause of it was that, though I thought very ill, I did not think quite so ill of Charles II. and his Ministry as they deserved. I imagined, too, that his Parliament would restrain him from engaging in such a war, or compel him to engage in our defence if France should attack us. These, I acknowledge, are excuses, not justifications. When the French marched into Holland and found it in a condition so unable to resist them, my fame as a Minister irrecoverably sank; for, not to appear a traitor, I was obliged to confess myself a dupe. But what praise is sufficient for the wisdom and virtue you showed in so firmly rejecting the offers which, I have been informed, were made to you, both by England and France, when first you appeared in arms at the head of your country, to give you the sovereignty of the Seven Provinces by the assistance and under the protection of the two Crowns! Believe me, great prince, had I been living in those times, and had known the generous answers you made to those offers (which were repeated more than once during the course of the war), not the most ancient and devoted servant to your family would have been more your friend than I. But who could reasonably hope for such moderation, and such a right sense of glory, in the mind of a young man descended from kings, whose mother was daughter to Charles I., and whose father had left him the seducing example of a very different conduct? Happy, indeed, was the English nation to have such a prince, so nearly allied to their Crown both in blood and by marriage, whom they might call to be their deliverer when bigotry and despotism, the two greatest enemies to human society, had almost overthrown their whole constitution in Church and State!

William. They might have been happy, but were not. As soon as I had accomplished their deliverance for them, many of them became my most implacable enemies, and even wished to restore the unforgiving prince whom they had so unanimously and so justly expelled from his kingdom. Such levity seems incredible. I could not myself have imagined it possible, in a nation famed for good sense, if I had not had proofs of it beyond contradiction. They seemed as much to forget what they called me over for as that they had called me over. The security of their religion, the maintenance of their liberty, were no longer their care. All was to yield to the incomprehensible doctrine of right divine and passive obedience. Thus the Tories grew Jacobites, after having renounced both that doctrine and King James, by their opposition to him, by their invitation of me, and by every Act of the Parliament which gave me the Crown. But the most troublesome of my enemies were a set of Republicans, who violently opposed all my measures, and joined with the Jacobites in disturbing my government, only because it was not a commonwealth.

De Witt. They who were Republicans under your government in the Kingdom of England did not love liberty, but aspired to dominion, and wished to throw the nation into a total confusion, that it might give them a chance of working out from that anarchy a better state for themselves.

William. Your observation is just. A proud man thinks himself a lover of liberty when he is only impatient of a power in government above his own, and were he a king, or the first Minister of a king, would be a tyrant. Nevertheless I will own to you, with the candour which becomes a virtuous prince, that there were in England some Whigs, and even some of the most sober and moderate Tories, who, with very honest intentions, and sometimes with good judgments, proposed new securities to the liberty of the nation, against the prerogative or influence of the Crown and the corruption of Ministers in future times. To some of these I gave way, being convinced they were right, but others I resisted for fear of weakening too much the royal authority, and breaking that balance in which consists the perfection of a mixed form of government. I should not, perhaps, have resisted so many if I had not seen in the House of Commons a disposition to rise in their demands on the Crown had they found it more yielding. The difficulties of my government, upon the whole, were so great that I once had determined, from mere disgust and resentment, to give back to the nation, assembled in Parliament, the crown they had placed on my head, and retire to Holland, where I found more affection and gratitude in the people. But I was stopped by the earnest supplications of my friends and by an unwillingness to undo the great work I had done, especially as I knew that, if England should return into the hands of King James, it would be impossible in that crisis to preserve the rest of Europe from the dominion of France.

De Witt. Heaven be praised that your Majesty did not persevere in so fatal a resolution! The United Provinces would have been ruined by it together with England. But I cannot enough express my astonishment that you should have met with such treatment as could suggest such a thought. The English must surely be a people incapable either of liberty or subjection.

William. There were, I must acknowledge, some faults in my temper and some in my government, which are an excuse for my subjects with regard to the uneasiness and disquiet they gave me. My taciturnity, which suited the genius of the Dutch, offended theirs. They love an affable prince; it was chiefly his affability that made them so fond of Charles II. Their frankness and good-humour could not brook the reserve and coldness of my nature. Then the excess of my favour to some of the Dutch, whom I had brought over with me, excited a national jealousy in the English and hurt their pride. My government also appeared, at last, too unsteady, too fluctuating between the Whigs and the Tories, which almost deprived me of the confidence and affection of both parties. I trusted too much to the integrity and the purity of my intentions, without using those arts that are necessary to allay the ferment of factions and allure men to their duty by soothing their passions. Upon the whole I am sensible that I better understood how to govern the Dutch than the English or the Scotch, and should probably have been thought a greater man if I had not been King of Great Britain.

De Witt. It is a shame to the English that gratitude and affection for such merit as yours were not able to overcome any little disgusts arising from your temper, and enthrone their deliverer in the hearts of his people. But will your Majesty give me leave to ask you one question? Is it true, as I have heard, that many of them disliked your alliances on the Continent and spoke of your war with France as a Dutch measure, in which you sacrificed England to Holland?

William. The cry of the nation at first was strong for the war, but before the end of it the Tories began publicly to talk the language you mention. And no wonder they did, for, as they then had a desire to set up again the maxims of government which had prevailed in the reign of their beloved Charles II., they could not but represent opposition to France, and vigorous measures taken to restrain her ambition, as unnecessary for England, because they well knew that the counsels of that king had been utterly averse to such measures; that his whole policy made him a friend to France; that he was governed by a French mistress, and even bribed by French money to give that Court his assistance, or at least his acquiescence, in all their designs.

De Witt. A King of England whose Cabinet is governed by France, and who becomes a vile pensioner to a French King, degrades himself from his royalty, and ought to be considered as an enemy to the nation. Indeed the whole policy of Charles II., when he was not forced off from his natural bias by the necessity he lay under of soothing his Parliament, was a constant, designed, systematical opposition to the interest of his people. His brother, though more sensible to the honour of England, was by his Popery and desire of arbitrary power constrained to lean upon France, and do nothing to obstruct her designs on the Continent or lessen her greatness. It was therefore necessary to place the British Crown on your head, not only with a view to preserve the religious and civil rights of the people from internal oppressions, but to rescue the whole State from that servile dependence on its natural enemy, which must unquestionably have ended in its destruction. What folly was it to revile your measures abroad, as sacrificing the interest of your British dominions to connections with the Continent, and principally with Holland! Had Great Britain no interest to hinder the French from being masters of all the Austrian Netherlands, and forcing the Seven United Provinces, her strongest barrier on the Continent against the power of that nation, to submit with the rest to their yoke? Would her trade, would her coasts, would her capital itself have been safe after so mighty an increase of shipping and sailors as France would have gained by those conquests? And what could have prevented them, but the war which you waged and the alliances which you formed? Could the Dutch and the Germans, unaided by Great Britain, have attempted to make head against a Power which, even with her assistance, strong and spirited as it was, they could hardly resist? And after the check which had been given to the encroachments of France by the efforts of the first grand alliance, did not a new and greater danger make it necessary to recur to another such league? Was not the union of France and Spain under one monarch, or even under one family, the most alarming contingency that ever had threatened the liberty of Europe?

William. I thought so, and I am sure I did not err in my judgment. But folly is blind, and faction wilfully shuts her eyes against the most evident truths that cross her designs, as she believes any lies, however palpable and absurd, that she thinks will assist them.

De Witt. The only objection which seems to have any real weight against your system of policy, with regard to the maintenance of a balance of power in Europe, is the enormous expense that must necessarily attend it; an expense which I am afraid neither England nor Holland will be able to bear without extreme inconvenience.

William. I will answer that objection by asking a question. If, when you were Pensionary of Holland, intelligence had been brought that the dykes were ready to break and the sea was coming in to overwhelm and to drown us, what would you have said to one of the deputies who, when you were proposing the proper repairs to stop the inundation, should have objected to the charge as too heavy on the Province? This was the case in a political sense with both England and Holland. The fences raised to keep out superstition and tyranny were all giving way; those dreadful evils were threatening, with their whole accumulated force, to break in upon us and overwhelm our ecclesiastical and civil constitutions. In such circumstances to object to a necessary expense is folly and madness.

De Witt. It is certain, sir, that the utmost abilities of a nation can never be so well employed as in the unwearied, pertinacious defence of their religion and freedom. When these are lost, there remains nothing that is worth the concern of a good or wise man. Nor do I think it consistent with the prudence of government not to guard against future dangers, as well as present; which precaution must be often in some degree expensive. I acknowledge, too, that the resources of a commercial country, which supports its trade, even in war, by invincible fleets, and takes care not to hurt it in the methods of imposing or collecting its taxes, are immense, and inconceivable till the trial is made; especially where the Government, which demands the supplies, is agreeable to the people. But yet an unlimited and continued expense will in the end be destructive. What matters it whether a State is mortally wounded by the hand of a foreign enemy, or dies by a consumption of its own vital strength? Such a consumption will come upon Holland sooner than upon England, because the latter has a greater radical force; but, great as it is, that force at last will be so diminished and exhausted by perpetual drains, that it may fail all at once, and those efforts, which may seem most surprisingly vigorous, will be in reality the convulsions of death. I don't apply this to your Majesty's government; but I speak with a view to what may happen hereafter from the extensive ideas of negotiation and war which you have established: they have been salutary to your kingdom; but they will, I fear, be pernicious in future times, if in pursuing great plans great Ministers do not act with a sobriety, prudence, and attention to frugality, which very seldom are joined with an extraordinary vigour and boldness of counsels.

DIALOGUE XIX. M. APICIUS - DARTENEUF.

Darteneuf. Alas! poor Apicius, I pity thee from my heart for not having lived in my age and in my country. How many good dishes, unknown at Rome in thy days, have I feasted upon in England!

Apicius. Keep your pity for yourself. How many good dishes have I feasted upon in Rome which England does not produce, or of which the knowledge has been lost, with other treasures of antiquity, in these degenerate days! The fat paps of a sow, the livers of scari, the brains of phoenicopters, and the tripotanum, which consisted of three excellent sorts of fish, for which you English have no names, the lupus marinus, the myxo, and the muraena.

Darteneuf. I thought the muraena had been our lamprey. We have delicate ones in the Severn.

Apicius. No; the muraena, so respected by the ancient Roman senators, was a salt-water fish, and kept by our nobles in ponds, into which the sea was admitted.

Darteneuf. Why, then, I dare say our Severn lampreys are better. Did you ever eat any of them stewed or potted?

Apicius. I was never in Britain. Your country then was too barbarous for me to go thither. I should have been afraid that the Britons would have eaten me.

Darteneuf. I am sorry for you, very sorry; for if you never were in Britain you never ate the best oysters.

Apicius. Pardon me, sir, your Sandwich oysters were brought to Rome in my time.

Darteneuf. They could not be fresh; they were good for nothing there. You should have come to Sandwich to eat them. It is a shame for you that you did not. An epicure talk of danger when he is in search of a dainty! Did not Leander swim over the Hellespont in a tempest to get to his mistress? And what is a wench to a barrel of exquisite oysters?

Apicius. Nay; I am sure you can't blame me for any want of alertness in seeking fine fishes. I sailed to the coast of Africa, from Minturnae in Campania, only to taste of one species, which I heard was larger there than it was on our coast; and finding that I had received a false information, I returned immediately, without even deigning to land.

Darteneuf. There was some sense in that. But why did not you also make a voyage to Sandwich? Had you once tasted those oysters in their highest perfection, you would never have come back; you would have eaten till you burst.

Apicius. I wish I had. It would have been better than poisoning myself, as I did at Rome, because I found, upon the balance of my accounts, I had only the pitiful sum of fourscore thousand pounds left, which would not afford me a table to keep me from starving.

Darteneuf. A sum of fourscore thousand pounds not keep you from starving! Would I had had it! I should have been twenty years in spending it, with the best table in London.

Apicius. Alas, poor man! This shows that you English have no idea of the luxury that reigned in our tables. Before I died I had spent in my kitchen 807,291 pounds 13s. 4d.

Darteneuf. I don't believe a word of it. There is certainly an error in the account.

Apicius. Why, the establishment of Lucullus for his suppers in the Apollo I mean for every supper he sat down to in the room which he called by that name was 5,000 drachms, which is in your money 1,614 pounds 11s. 8d.

Darteneuf. Would I had supped with him there! But are you sure there is no blunder in these calculations?

Apicius. Ask your learned men that. I reckon as they tell me. But you may think that these feasts were made only by great men, by triumphant generals, like Lucullus, who had plundered all Asia to help him in his housekeeping. What will you say when I tell you that the player AEsopus had one dish that cost him 6,000 sestertia, that is, 4,843 pounds 10s. English?

Darteneuf. What will I say? Why, that I pity my worthy friend Mr. Gibber, and that, if I had known this when alive, I should have hanged myself for vexation that I did not live in those days.

Apicius. Well you might, well you might. You don't know what eating is. You never could know it. Nothing less than the wealth of the Roman Empire is sufficient to enable a man of taste to keep a good table. Our players were infinitely richer than your princes.

Darteneuf. Oh that I had but lived in the blessed reign of Caligula, or of Vitellius, or of Heliogabalus, and had been admitted to the honour of dining with their slaves!

Apicius. Ay, there you touch me. I am miserable that I died before their good times. They carried the glories of their table much farther than the best eaters of the age in which I lived. Vitellius spent in feasting, within the compass of one year, what would amount in your money to above 7,200,000 pounds. He told me so himself in a conversation I had with him not long ago. And the two others you mentioned did not fall very short of his royal magnificence.

Darteneuf. These, indeed, were great princes. But what most affects me is the luxury of that upstart fellow AEsopus. Pray, of what ingredients might the dish he paid so much for consist?

Apicius. Chiefly of singing birds. It was that which so greatly enhanced the price.

Darteneuf. Of singing birds! Choke him! I never ate but one, which I stole out of its cage from a lady of my acquaintance, and all London was in an uproar, as if I had stolen and roasted an only child. But, upon recollection, I doubt whether I have really so much cause to envy AEsopus. For the singing bird which I ate was not so good as a wheat-ear or becafigue. And therefore I suspect that all the luxury you have bragged of was nothing but vanity. It was like the foolish extravagance of the son of AEsopus, who dissolved pearls in vinegar and drank them at supper. I will stake my credit that a haunch of good buck venison and my favourite ham pie were much better dishes than any at the table of Vitellius himself. It does not appear that you ancients ever had any good soups, without which a man of taste cannot possibly dine. The rabbits in Italy are detestable. But what is better than the wing of one of our English wild rabbits? I have been told you had no turkeys. The mutton in Italy is ill-flavoured. And as for your boars roasted whole, they were only fit to be served up at a corporation feast or election dinner. A small barbecued hog is worth a hundred of them. And a good collar of Canterbury or Shrewsbury brawn is a much better dish.

Apicius. If you had some meats that we wanted, yet our cookery must have been greatly superior to yours. Our cooks were so excellent that they could give to hog's flesh the taste of all other meats.

Darteneuf. I should never have endured their imitations. You might as easily have imposed on a good connoisseur in painting the copy of a fine picture for the original. Our cooks, on the contrary, give to all other meats, and even to some kinds of fish, a rich flavour of bacon without destroying that which makes the distinction of one from another. It does not appear to me that essence of hams was ever known to the ancients. We have a hundred ragouts, the composition of which surpasses all description. Had yours been as good, you could not have lain indolently lolling upon couches while you were eating. They would have made you sit up and mind your business. Then you had a strange custom of hearing things read to you while you were at supper. This demonstrates that you were not so well entertained as we are with our meat. When I was at table, I neither heard, nor saw, nor spoke; I only tasted. But the worst of all is that, in the utmost perfection of your luxury, you had no wine to be named with claret, Burgundy, champagne, old hock, or Tokay. You boasted much of your Falernum, but I have tasted the Lachrymae Christi and other wines of that coast, not one of which would I have drunk above a glass or two of if you would have given me the Kingdom of Naples. I have read that you boiled your wines and mixed water with them, which is sufficient evidence that in themselves they were not fit to drink.

Apicius. I am afraid you do really excel us in wines; not to mention your beer, your cider, and your perry, of all which I have heard great fame from your countrymen, and their report has been confirmed by the testimony of their neighbours who have travelled into England. Wonderful things have been also said to me of an English liquor called punch.

Darteneuf. Ay, to have died without tasting that is miserable indeed! There is rum punch and arrack punch! It is difficult to say which is best, but Jupiter would have given his nectar for either of them, upon my word and honour.

Apicius. The thought of them puts me into a fever with thirst.

Darteneuf. Those incomparable liquors are brought to us from the East and West Indies, of the first of which you knew little, and of the latter nothing. This alone is sufficient to determine the dispute. What a new world of good things for eating and drinking has Columbus opened to us! Think of that, and despair.

Apicius. I cannot indeed but exceedingly lament my ill fate that America was not discovered before I was born. It tortures me when I hear of chocolate, pineapples, and a number of other fine fruits, or delicious meats, produced there which I have never tasted.

Darteneuf. The single advantage of having sugar to sweeten everything with, instead of honey, which you, for want of the other, were obliged to make use of, is inestimable.

Apicius. I confess your superiority in that important article. But what grieves me most is that I never ate a turtle. They tell me that it is absolutely the best of all foods.

Darteneuf. Yes, I have heard the Americans say so, but I never ate any; for in my time they were not brought over to England.

Apicius. Never ate any turtle! How couldst thou dare to accuse me of not going to Sandwich to eat oysters, and didst not thyself take a trip to America to riot on turtles? But know, wretched man, I am credibly informed that they are now as plentiful in England as sturgeons. There are turtle-boats that go regularly to London and Bristol from the West Indies. I have just received this information from a fat alderman, who died in London last week of a surfeit he got at a turtle feast in that city.

Darteneuf. What does he say? Does he affirm to you that turtle is better than venison?

Apicius. He says, there was a haunch of the fattest venison untouched, while every mouth was employed on the turtle alone.

Darteneuf. Alas! how imperfect is human felicity! I lived in an age when the noble science of eating was supposed to have been carried to its highest perfection in England and France. And yet a turtle feast is a novelty to me! Would it be impossible, do you think, to obtain leave from Pluto of going back for one day to my own table at London just to taste of that food? I would promise to kill myself by the quantity of it I would eat before the next morning.

Apicius. You have forgot you have no body. That which you had has long been rotten, and you can never return to the earth with another, unless Pythagoras should send you thither to animate a hog. But comfort yourself that, as you have eaten dainties which I never tasted, so the next age will eat some unknown to this. New discoveries will be made, and new delicacies brought from other parts of the world. But see; who comes hither? I think it is Mercury.

Mercury. Gentlemen, I must tell you that I have stood near you invisible, and heard your discourse, a privilege which, you know, we deities use as often as we please. Attend, therefore, to what I shall communicate to you, relating to the subject upon which you have been talking. I know two men, one of whom lived in ancient, and the other in modern times, who had much more pleasure in eating than either of you through the whole course of your lives.

Apicius. One of these happy epicures, I presume, was a Sybarite, and the other a French gentleman settled in the West Indies.

Mercury. No; one was a Spartan soldier, and the other an English farmer. I see you both look astonished. But what I tell you is truth. Labour and hunger gave a relish to the black broth of the former, and the salt beef of the latter, beyond what you ever found in the tripotanums or ham pies, that vainly stimulated your forced and languid appetites, which perpetual indolence weakened, and constant luxury overcharged.

Darteneuf. This, Apicius, is more mortifying than not to have shared a turtle feast.

Apicius. I wish, Mercury, you had taught me your art of cookery in my lifetime; but it is a sad thing not to know what good living is till after one is dead.

DIALOGUE XX. ALEXANDER THE GREAT - CHARLES XII., KING OF SWEDEN.

Alexander. Your Majesty seems in great wrath! Who has offended you?

Charles. The offence is to you as much as me. Here is a fellow admitted into Elysium who has affronted us both, an English poet, one Pope. He has called us two madmen!

Alexander. I have been unlucky in poets. No prince ever was fonder of the Muses than I, or has received from them a more ungrateful return. When I was alive, I declared that I envied Achilles because he had a Homer to celebrate his exploits; and I most bountifully rewarded Choerilus, a pretender to poetry, for writing verses on mine. But my liberality, instead of doing me honour, has since drawn upon me the ridicule of Horace, a witty Roman poet; and Lucan, another versifier of the same nation, has loaded my memory with the harshest invectives.

Charles. I know nothing of these; but I know that in my time a pert French satirist, one Boileau, made so free with your character, that I tore his book for having abused my favourite hero. And now this saucy Englishman has libelled us both. But I have a proposal to make to you for the reparation of our honour. If you will join with me, we will turn all these insolent scribblers out of Elysium, and throw them down headlong to the bottom of Tartarus, in spite of Pluto and all his guards.

Alexander. This is just such a scheme as that you formed at Bender, to maintain yourself there, with the aid of three hundred Swedes, against the whole force of the Ottoman Empire. And I must say that such follies gave the English poet too much cause to call you a madman.

Charles. If my heroism was madness, yours, I presume, was not wisdom.

Alexander. There was a vast difference between your conduct and mine. Let poets or declaimers say what they will, history shows that I was not only the bravest soldier, but one of the ablest commanders the world has ever seen. Whereas you, by imprudently leading your army into vast and barren deserts at the approach of the winter, exposed it to perish in its march for want of subsistence, lost your artillery, lost a great number of your soldiers, and was forced to fight with the Muscovites under such disadvantages as made it almost impossible for you to conquer.

Charles. I will not dispute your superiority as a general. It is not for me, a mere mortal, to contend with the son of Jupiter Ammon.

Alexander. I suppose you think my pretending that Jupiter was my father as much entitles me to the name of a madman as your extravagant behaviour at Bender does you. But you are greatly mistaken. It was not my vanity, but my policy, which set up that pretension. When I proposed to undertake the conquest of Asia, it was necessary for me to appear to the people something more than a man. They had been used to the idea of demi-god heroes. I therefore claimed an equal descent with Osiris and Sesostris, with Bacchus and Hercules, the former conquerors of the East. The opinion of my divinity assisted my arms and subdued all nations before me, from the Granicus to the Ganges. But though I called myself the son of Jupiter, and kept up the veneration that name inspired, by a courage which seemed more than human, and by the sublime magnanimity of all my behaviour, I did not forget that I was the son of Philip. I used the policy of my father and the wise lessons of Aristotle, whom he had made my preceptor, in the conduct of all my great designs. It was the son of Philip who planted Greek colonies in Asia as far as the Indies; who formed projects of trade more extensive than his empire itself; who laid the foundations of them in the midst of his wars; who built Alexandria, to be the centre and staple of commerce between Europe, Asia, and Africa, who sent Nearchus to navigate the unknown Indian seas, and intended to have gone himself from those seas to the Pillars of Hercules, that is, to have explored the passage round Africa, the discovery of which has since been so glorious to Vasco de Gama. It was the son of Philip who, after subduing the Persians, governed them with such lenity, such justice, and such wisdom, that they loved him even more than ever they had loved their natural kings; and who, by intermarriages and all methods that could best establish a coalition between the conquerors and the conquered, united them into one people. But what, sir, did you do to advance the trade of your subjects, to procure any benefit to those you had vanquished, or to convert any enemy into a friend?

Charles. When I might easily have made myself King of Poland, and was advised to do so by Count Piper, my favourite Minister, I generously gave that kingdom to Stanislas, as you had given a great part of you conquests in India to Porus, besides his own dominions, which you restored to him entire after you had beaten his army and taken him captive.

Alexander. I gave him the government of those countries under me and as my lieutenant, which was the best method of preserving my power in conquests where I could not leave garrisons sufficient to maintain them. The same policy was afterwards practised by the Romans, who of all conquerors, except me, were the greatest politicians. But neither was I nor were they so extravagant as to conquer only for others, or dethrone kings with no view but merely to have the pleasure of bestowing their crowns on some of their subjects without any advantage to ourselves. Nevertheless, I will own that my expedition to India was an exploit of the son of Jupiter, not of the son of Philip. I had done better if I had stayed to give more consistency to my Persian and Grecian Empires, instead of attempting new conquests and at such a distance so soon. Yet even this war was of use to hinder my troops from being corrupted by the effeminacy of Asia, and to keep up that universal awe of my name which in those countries was the great support of my power.

Charles. In the unwearied activity with which I proceeded from one enterprise to another, I dare call myself your equal. Nay, I may pretend to a higher glory than you, because you only went on from victory to victory; but the greatest losses were not able to diminish my ardour or stop the efforts of my daring and invincible spirit.

Alexander. You showed in adversity much more magnanimity than you did in prosperity. How unworthy of a prince who imitated me was your behaviour to the king your arms had vanquished! The compelling Augustus to write himself a letter of congratulation to one of his vassals whom you had placed in his throne, was the very reverse of my treatment of Porus and Darius. It was an ungenerous insult upon his ill-fortune. It was the triumph of a little and a low mind. The visit you made him immediately after that insult was a further contempt, offensive to him, and both useless and dangerous to yourself.

Charles. I feared no danger from it. I knew he durst not use the power I gave him to hurt me.

Alexander. If his resentment in that instant had prevailed over his fear, as it was likely to do, you would have perished deservedly by your insolence and presumption. For my part, intrepid as I was in all dangers which I thought it was necessary or proper for me to meet, I never put myself one moment in the power of an enemy whom I had offended. But you had the rashness of folly as well as of heroism. A false opinion conceived of your enemy's weakness proved at last your undoing. When, in answer to some reasonable propositions of peace sent to you by the Czar, you said, "You would come and treat with him at Moscow," he replied very justly, "That you affected to act like Alexander, but should not find in him a Darius." And, doubtless, you ought to have been better acquainted with the character of that prince. Had Persia been governed by a Peter Alexowitz when I made war against it, I should have acted more cautiously, and not have counted so much on the superiority of my troops in valour and discipline over an army commanded by a king who was so capable of instructing them in all they wanted.

Charles. The battle of Narva, won by eight thousand Swedes against fourscore thousand Muscovites, seemed to authorise my contempt of the nation and their prince.

Alexander. It happened that their prince was not present in that battle. But he had not as yet had the time which was necessary to instruct his barbarous soldiers. You gave him that time, and he made so good a use of it that you found at Pultowa the Muscovites become a different nation. If you had followed the blow you gave them at Narva, and marched directly to Moscow, you might have destroyed their Hercules in his cradle. But you suffered him to grow till his strength was mature, and then acted as if he had been still in his childhood.

Charles. I must confess you excelled me in conduct, in policy, and in true magnanimity. But my liberality was not inferior to yours; and neither you nor any mortal ever surpassed me in the enthusiasm of courage. I was also free from those vices which sullied your character. I never was drunk; I killed no friend in the riot of a feast; I fired no palace at the instigation of a harlot.

Alexander. It may perhaps be admitted, as some excuse for my drunkenness, that the Persians esteemed it an excellence in their kings to be able to drink a great quantity of wine, and the Macedonians were far from thinking it a dishonour. But you were as frantic and as cruel when sober as I was when drunk. You were sober when you resolved to continue in Turkey against the will of your host, the Grand Signor. You were sober when you commanded the unfortunate Patkull, whose only crime was his having maintained the liberties of his country, and who bore the sacred character of an ambassador, to be broken alive on the wheel, against the laws of nations, and those of humanity, more inviolable still to a generous mind. You were likewise sober when you wrote to the Senate of Sweden, who, upon a report of your death, endeavoured to take some care of your kingdom, that you would send them one of your boots, and from that they should receive their orders if they pretended to meddle in government, an insult much worse than any the Macedonians complained of from me when I was most heated with wine and with adulation. As for my chastity, it was not so perfect as yours, though on some occasions I obtained great praise for my continence; but, perhaps, if you had been not quite so insensible to the charms of the fair sex, it would have mitigated and softened the fierceness, the pride, and the obstinacy of your nature.

Charles. It would have softened me into a woman, or, what I think still more contemptible, the slave of a woman. But you seem to insinuate that you never were cruel or frantic unless when you were drunk. This I absolutely deny. You were not drunk when you crucified Hephaestion's physician for not curing a man who killed himself by his intemperance in his sickness, nor when you sacrificed to the manes of that favourite officer the whole nation of the Cusseans, men, women, and children, who were entirely innocent of his death because you had read in Homer that Achilles had immolated some Trojan captives on the tomb of Patroclus. I could mention other proofs that your passions inflamed you as much as wine, but these are sufficient.

Alexander. I can't deny that my passions were sometimes so violent as to deprive me for a while of the use of my reason; especially when the pride of such amazing successes, the servitude of the Persians, and barbarian flattery had intoxicated my mind. To bear at my age, with continual moderation, such fortune as mine, was hardly in human nature. As for you, there was an excess and intemperance in your virtues which turned them all into vices. And one virtue you wanted, which in a prince is very commendable and beneficial to the public, I mean, the love of science and of the elegant arts. Under my care and patronage they were carried in Greece to their utmost perfection. Aristotle, Apelles, and Lysippus were among the glories of my reign. Yours was illustrated only by battles. Upon the whole, though, from some resemblance between us I should naturally be inclined to decide in your favour, yet I must give the priority in renown to your enemy, Peter Alexowitz. That great monarch raised his country; you ruined yours. He was a legislator; you were a tyrant.

DIALOGUE XXI. CARDINAL XIMENES - CARDINAL WOLSEY.

Wolsey. You seem to look on me, Ximenes, with an air of superiority, as if I was not your equal. Have you forgotten that I was the favourite and first Minister of a great King of England? that I was at once Lord High Chancellor, Bishop of Durham, Bishop of Winchester, Archbishop of York, and Cardinal Legate? On what other subject were ever accumulated so many dignities, such honours, such power?

Ximenes. In order to prove yourself my equal, you are pleased to tell me what you had, not what you did. But it is not the having great offices, it is the doing great things, that makes a great Minister. I know that for some years you governed the mind of King Henry VIII., and consequently his kingdom, with the most absolute sway. Let me ask you, then, What were the acts of your reign?

Wolsey. My acts were those of a very skilful courtier and able politician. I managed a temper which nature had made the most difficult to manage of any perhaps that ever existed, with such consummate address that all its passions were rendered entirely subservient to my inclinations. In foreign affairs I turned the arms of my master or disposed of his friendship, whichever way my own interest happened to direct. It was not with him, but with me, that treaties were made by the Emperor or by France; and none were concluded during my Ministry that did not contain some Article in my favour, besides secret assurances of aiding my ambition or resentment, which were the real springs of all my negotiations. At home I brought the pride of the English nobility, which had resisted the greatest of the Plantagenets, to bow submissively to the son of a butcher of Ipswich. And, as my power was royal, my state and magnificence were suitable to it; my buildings, my furniture, my household, my equipage, my liberalities, and my charities were above the rank of a subject.

Ximenes. From all you have said I understand that you gained great advantages for yourself in the course of your Ministry, too great, indeed, for a good man to desire, or a wise man to accept. But what did you do for your sovereign and for the State? You make me no answer. What I did is well known. I was not content with forcing the arrogance of the Spanish nobility to stoop to my power, but used that power to free the people from their oppressions. In you they respected the royal authority; I made them respect the majesty of the laws. I also relieved my countrymen, the commons of Castile, from a most grievous burden, by an alteration in the method of collecting their taxes. After the death of Isabella I preserved the tranquillity of Aragon and Castile by procuring the regency of the latter for Ferdinand, a wise and valiant prince, though he had not been my friend during the life of the queen. And when after his decease I was raised to the regency by the general esteem and affection of the Castilians, I administered the government with great courage, firmness, and prudence; with the most perfect disinterestedness in regard to myself, and most zealous concern for the public. I suppressed all the factions which threatened to disturb the peace of that kingdom in the minority and the absence of the young king; and prevented the discontents of the commons of Castile, too justly incensed against the Flemish Ministers, who governed their prince and rapaciously pillaged their country, from breaking out during my life into open rebellion, as they did, most unhappily, soon after my death. These were my civil acts; but, to complete the renown of my administration, I added to it the palm of military glory. At my own charges, and myself commanding the army, I conquered Oran from the Moors, and annexed it, with its territory, to the Spanish dominions.

Wolsey. My soul was as elevated and noble as yours, my understanding as strong, and more refined; but the difference of our conduct arose from the difference of our objects. To raise your reputation and secure your power in Castile, by making that kingdom as happy and as great as you could, was your object. Mine was to procure the Triple Crown for myself by the assistance of my sovereign and of the greatest foreign Powers. Each of us took the means that were evidently most proper to the accomplishment of his ends.

Ximenes. Can you confess such a principle of your conduct without a blush? But you will at least be ashamed that you failed in your purpose, and were the dupe of the Powers with whom you negotiated, after having dishonoured the character of your master in order to serve your own ambition. I accomplished my desire with glory to my sovereign and advantage to my country. Besides this difference, there was a great one in the methods by which we acquired our power. We both owed it, indeed, to the favour of princes; but I gained Isabella's by the opinion she had of my piety and integrity. You gained Henry's by a complaisance and course of life which were a reproach to your character and sacred orders.

Wolsey. I did not, as you, Ximenes, did, carry with me to Court the austerity of a monk; nor, if I had done so, could I possibly have gained any influence there. Isabella and Henry were different characters, and their favour was to be sought in different ways. By making myself agreeable to the latter, I so governed his passions, unruly as they were, that while I lived they did not produce any of those dreadful effects which after my death were caused by them in his family and kingdom.

Ximenes. If Henry VIII., your master, had been King of Castile, I would never have been drawn by him out of my cloister. A man of virtue and spirit will not be prevailed with to go into a Court where he cannot rise without baseness.

Wolsey. The inflexibility of your mind had like to have ruined you in some of your measures; and the bigotry which you had derived from your long abode in a cloister, and retained when a Minister, was very near depriving the Crown of Castile of the new-conquered kingdom of Granada by the revolt of the Moors in that city, whom you had prematurely forced to change their religion. Do you not remember how angry King Ferdinand was with you on that account?

Ximenes. I do, and must acknowledge that my zeal was too intemperate in all that proceeding.

Wolsey. My worst complaisances to King Henry VIII. were far less hurtful to England than the unjust and inhuman Court of Inquisition, which you established in Granada to watch over the faith of your unwilling converts, has been to Spain.

Ximenes. I only revived and settled in Granada an ancient tribunal, instituted first by one of our saints against the Albigenses, and gave it greater powers. The mischiefs which have attended it cannot be denied; but if any force may be used for the maintenance of religion (and the Church of Rome has, you know, declared authoritatively that it may) none could be so effectual to answer the purpose.

Wolsey. This is an argument rather against the opinion of the Church than for the Inquisition. I will only say I think myself very happy that my administration was stained with no action of cruelty, not even cruelty sanctified by the name of religion. My temper indeed, which influenced my conduct more than my principles, was much milder than yours. To the proud I was proud, but to my friends and inferiors benevolent and humane. Had I succeeded in the great object of my ambition, had I acquired the Popedom, I should have governed the Church with more moderation and better sense than probably you would have done if you had exchanged the See of Toledo for that of Rome. My good-nature, my policy, my taste for magnificence, my love of the fine arts, of wit, and of learning, would have made me the delight of all the Italians, and have given me a rank among the greatest princes. Whereas in you the sour bigot and rigid monk would too much have prevailed over the prince and the statesman.

Ximenes. What either of us would have been in that situation does not appear; but, if you are compared to me as a Minister, you are vastly inferior. The only circumstance in which you can justly pretend to any equality is the encouragement you gave to learning and your munificence in promoting it, which was indeed very great. Your two colleges founded at Ipswich and Oxford may vie with my University at Alcala de Henara. But in our generosity there was this difference, all my revenues were spent in well-placed liberalities, in acts of charity, piety, and virtue; whereas a great part of your enormous wealth was squandered away in luxury and vain ostentation. With regard to all other points, my superiority is apparent. You were only a favourite; I was the friend and the father of the people. You served yourself; I served the State. The conclusion of our lives was also much more honourable to me than you.

Wolsey. Did not you die, as I did, in disgrace with your master?

Ximenes. That disgrace was brought upon me by a faction of foreigners, to whose power, as a good Spaniard, I would not submit. A Minister who falls a victim to such an opposition rises by his fall. Yours was not graced by any public cause, any merit to the nation. Your spirit, therefore, sank under it; you bore it with meanness. Mine was unbroken, superior to my enemies, superior to fortune, and I died, as I had lived, with undiminished dignity and greatness of mind.

DIALOGUE XXII. LUCIAN - RABELAIS.

Lucian. Friend Rabelais, well met, our souls are very good company for one another; we both were great wits and most audacious freethinkers. We laughed often at folly, and sometimes at wisdom. I was, indeed, more correct and more elegant in my style; but then, in return, you had a greater fertility of imagination. My "True History" is much inferior, in fancy and invention, in force of wit and keenness of satire, to your "History of the Acts of Gargantua and Pantagruel."

Rabelais. You do me great honour; but I may say, without vanity, that both those compositions entitle the authors of them to a very distinguished place among memoir-writers, travellers, and even historians, ancient and modern.

Lucian. Doubtless they do; but will you pardon me if I ask you one question? Why did you choose to write such absolute nonsense as you have in some places of your illustrious work?

Rabelais. I was forced to compound my physic for the mind with a large dose of nonsense in order to make it go down. To own the truth to you, if I had not so frequently put on the fool's-cap, the freedoms I took in other places with cowls, with Red Hats, and the Triple Crown itself, would have brought me into great danger. Not only my book, but I myself, should, in all probability, have been condemned to the flames; and martyrdom was an honour to which I never aspired. I therefore counterfeited folly, like Junius Brutus, from the wisest of all principles, that of self-preservation. You, Lucian, had no need to use so much caution. Your heathen priests desired only a sacrifice now and then from an Epicurean as a mark of conformity, and kindly allowed him to make as free as he pleased, in conversation or writings, with the whole tribe of gods and goddesses, from the thundering Jupiter and the scolding Juno, down to the dog Anubis and the fragrant dame Cloacina.

Lucian. Say rather that our Government allowed us that liberty; for I assure you our priests were by no means pleased with it, at least, they were not in my time.

Rabelais. The wiser men they; for, in spite of the conformity required by the laws and enforced by the magistrate, that ridicule brought the system of pagan theology into contempt, not only with the philosophical part of mankind, but even with the vulgar.

Lucian. It did so, and the ablest defenders of paganism were forced to give up the poetical fables and allegorise the whole.

Rabelais. An excellent way of drawing sense out of absurdity, and grave instructions from lewdness. There is a great modern wit, Sir Francis Bacon, Lord Verulam, who in his treatise entitled "The Wisdom of the Ancients" has done more for you that way than all your own priests.

Lucian. He has indeed shown himself an admirable chemist, and made a fine transmutation of folly into wisdom. But all the later Platonists took the same method of defending our faith when it was attacked by the Christians; and certainly a more judicious one could not be found. Our fables say that in one of their wars with the Titans the gods were defeated, and forced to turn themselves into beasts in order to escape from the conquerors. Just the reverse happened here, for by this happy art our beastly divinities were turned again into rational beings.

Rabelais. Give me a good commentator, with a subtle, refining, philosophical head, and you shall have the edification of seeing him draw the most sublime allegories and the most venerable mystic truths from my history of the noble Gargantua and Pantagruel. I don't despair of being proved, to the entire satisfaction of some future ape, to have been, without exception, the profoundest divine and metaphysician that ever yet held a pen.

Lucian. I shall rejoice to see you advanced to that honour. But in the meantime I may take the liberty to consider you as one of our class. There you sit very high.

Rabelais. I am afraid there is another, and a modern author too, whom you would bid to sit above me, and but just below yourself, I mean Dr. Swift.

Lucian. It was not necessary for him to throw so much nonsense into his history of Lemuel Gulliver as you did into that of your two illustrious heroes; and his style is far more correct than yours. His wit never descended, as yours frequently did, into the lowest of taverns, nor ever wore the meanest garb of the vulgar.

Rabelais. If the garb which it wore was not as mean, I am certain it was sometimes as dirty as mine.

Lucian. It was not always nicely clean; yet, in comparison with you, he was decent and elegant. But whether there was not in your compositions more fire, and a more comic spirit, I will not determine.

Rabelais. If you will not determine it, e'en let it remain a matter in dispute, as I have left the great question, Whether Panurge should marry or not? I would as soon undertake to measure the difference between the height and bulk of the giant Gargantua and his Brobdignagian Majesty, as the difference of merit between my writings and Swift's. If any man takes a fancy to like my book, let him freely enjoy the entertainment it gives him, and drink to my memory in a bumper. If another likes Gulliver, let him toast Dr. Swift. Were I upon earth I would pledge him in a bumper, supposing the wine to be good. If a third likes neither of us, let him silently pass the bottle and be quiet.

Lucian. But what if he will not be quiet? A critic is an unquiet creature.

Rabelais. Why, then he will disturb himself, not me.

Lucian. You are a greater philosopher than I thought you. I knew you paid no respect to Popes or kings, but to pay none to critics is, in an author, a magnanimity beyond all example.

Rabelais. My life was a farce; my death was a farce; and would you have me make my book a serious affair? As for you, though in general you are only a joker, yet sometimes you must be ranked among grave authors. You have written sage and learned dissertations on history and other weighty matters. The critics have therefore an undoubted right to maul you; they find you in their province. But if any of them dare to come into mine, I will order Gargantua to swallow them up, as he did the six pilgrims, in the next salad he eats.

Lucian. Have I not heard that you wrote a very good serious book on the aphorisms of Hippocrates?

Rabelais. Upon my faith I had forgot it. I am so used to my fool's coat that I don't know myself in my solemn doctor's gown. But your information was right; that book was indeed a very respectable work. Yet nobody reads it; and if I had writ nothing else, I should have been reckoned, at best, a lackey to Hippocrates, whereas the historian of Panurge is an eminent writer. Plain good sense, like a dish of solid beef or mutton, is proper only for peasants; but a ragout of folly, well dressed with a sharp sauce of wit, is fit to be served up at an emperor's table.

Lucian. You are an admirable pleasant fellow. Let me embrace you. How Apollo and the Muses may rank you on Parnassus I am not very certain; but, if I were Master of the Ceremonies on Mount Olympus, you should be placed, with a full bowl of nectar before you, at the right hand of Momus.

Rabelais. I wish you were; but I fear the inhabitants of those sublime regions will like your company no better than mine. Indeed, how Momus himself could get a seat at that table I can't well comprehend. It has been usual, I confess, in some of our Courts upon earth, to have a privileged jester, called the king's fool. But in the Court of Heaven one should not have supposed such an officer as Jupiter's fool. Your allegorical theology in this point is very abstruse.

Lucian. I think our priests admitted Momus into our heaven, as the Indians are said to worship the devil, through fear. They had a mind to keep fair with him. For we may talk of the giants as much as we please, but to our gods there is no enemy so formidable as he. Ridicule is the terror of all false religion. Nothing but truth can stand its lash.

Rabelais. Truth, advantageously set in a good and fair light, can stand any attacks; but those of Ridicule are so teasing and so fallacious that I have seen them put her ladyship very much out of humour.

Lucian. Ay, friend Rabelais, and sometimes out of countenance too. But Truth and Wit in confederacy will strike Momus dumb. United they are invincible, and such a union is necessary upon certain occasions. False Reasoning is most effectually exposed by Plain Sense; but Wit is the best opponent to False Ridicule, as Just Ridicule is to all the absurdities which dare to assume the venerable names of Philosophy or Religion. Had we made such a proper use of our agreeable talents; had we employed our ridicule to strip the foolish faces of Superstition, Fanaticism, and Dogmatical Pride of the serious and solemn masks with which they are covered, at the same time exerting all the sharpness of our wit to combat the flippancy and pertness of those who argue only by jests against reason and evidence in points of the highest and most serious concern, we should have much better merited the esteem of mankind.

DIALOGUE XXIII. PERICLES - COSMO DE MEDICIS, THE FIRST OF THAT NAME.

Pericles. In what I have heard of your character and your fortune, illustrious Cosmo, I find a most remarkable resemblance with mine. We both lived in republics where the sovereign power was in the people; and by mere civil arts, but more especially by our eloquence, attained, without any force, to such a degree of authority that we ruled those tumultuous and stormy democracies with an absolute sway, turned the tempests which agitated them upon the heads of our enemies, and after having long and prosperously conducted the greatest affairs in war and peace, died revered and lamented by all our fellow-citizens.

Cosmo. We have indeed an equal right to value ourselves on that noblest of empires, the empire we gained over the minds of our countrymen. Force or caprice may give power, but nothing can give a lasting authority except wisdom and virtue. By these we obtained, by these we preserved, in our respective countries, a dominion unstained by usurpation or blood, a dominion conferred on us by the public esteem and the public affection. We were in reality sovereigns, while we lived with the simplicity of private men; and Athens and Florence believed themselves to be free, though they obeyed all our dictates. This is more than was done by Philip of Macedon, or Sylla, or Caesar. It is the perfection of policy to tame the fierce spirit of popular liberty, not by blows or by chains, but by soothing it into a voluntary obedience, and bringing it to lick the hand that restrains it.

Pericles. The task can never be easy, but the difficulty was still greater to me than to you. For I had a lion to tame, from whose intractable fury the greatest men of my country, and of the whole world, with all their wisdom and virtue, could not save themselves. Themistocles and Aristides were examples of terror that might well have deterred me from the administration of public affairs at Athens. Another impediment in my way was the power of Cimon, who for his goodness, his liberality, and the lustre of his victories over the Persians was much beloved by the people, and at the same time, by being thought to favour aristocracy, had all the noble and rich citizens devoted to his party. It seemed impossible to shake so well established a greatness. Yet by the charms and force of my eloquence, which exceeded that of all orators contemporary with me; by the integrity of my life, my moderation, and my prudence; but, above all, by my artful management of the people, whose power I increased that I might render it the basis and support of my own, I gained such an ascendant over all my opponents that, having first procured the banishment of Cimon by ostracism, and then of Thucydides, another formidable antagonist set up by the nobles against my authority, I became the unrivalled chief, or rather the monarch, of the Athenian Republic, without ever putting to death, in above forty years that my administration continued, one of my fellow-citizens; a circumstance which I declared, when I lay on my death-bed, to be, in my own judgment, more honourable to me than all my prosperity in the government of the State, or the nine trophies erected for so many victories obtained by my conduct.

Cosmo. I had also the same happiness to boast of at my death. And some additions were made to the territories of Florence under my government; but I myself was no soldier, and the Commonwealth I directed was never either so warlike or so powerful as Athens. I must, therefore, not pretend to vie with you in the lustre of military glory; and I will moreover acknowledge that, to govern a people whose spirit and pride were exalted by the wonderful victories of Marathon, Mycale, Salamis, and Plataea, was much more difficult than to rule the Florentines and the Tuscans. The liberty of the Athenians was in your time more imperious, more haughty, more insolent, than the despotism of the King of Persia. How great, then, must have been your ability and address that could so absolutely reduce it under your power! Yet the temper of my countrymen was not easy to govern, for it was exceedingly factious. The history of Florence is little else, for several ages, than an account of conspiracies against the State. In my youth I myself suffered much by the dissensions which then embroiled the Republic. I was imprisoned and banished, but after the course of some years my enemies, in their turn, were driven into exile. I was brought back in triumph, and from that time till my death, which was above thirty years, I governed the Florentines, not by arms or evil arts of tyrannical power, but with a legal authority, which I exercised so discreetly as to gain the esteem of all the neighbouring potentates, and such a constant affection of all my fellow-citizens that an inscription, which gave me the title of Father of my Country, was engraved on my monument by an unanimous decree of the whole Commonwealth.

Pericles. Your end was incomparably more happy than mine. For you died rather of age than any violent illness, and left the Florentines in a state of peace and prosperity procured for them by your counsels. But I died of the plague, after having seen it almost depopulate Athens, and left my country engaged in a most dangerous war, to which my advice and the power of my eloquence had excited the people. The misfortune of the pestilence, with the inconveniences they suffered on account of the war, so irritated their minds, that not long before my death they condemned me to a fine.

Cosmo. It is wonderful that, when once their anger was raised, it went no further against you! A favourite of the people, when disgraced, is in still greater danger than a favourite of a king.

Pericles. Your surprise will increase at hearing that very soon afterwards they chose me their general, and conferred on me again the principal direction of all their affairs. Had I lived I should have so conducted the war as to have ended it with advantage and honour to my country. For, having secured to her the sovereignty of the sea by the defeat of the Samians, before I let her engage with the power of Sparta, I knew that our enemies would be at length wearied out and compelled to sue for a peace, because the city, from the strength of its fortifications and the great army within it, being on the land side impregnable to the Spartans, and drawing continual supplies from the sea, suffered not much by their ravages of the country about it, from whence I had before removed all the inhabitants; whereas their allies were undone by the descents we made on their coasts.

Cosmo. You seem to have understood beyond all other men what advantages are to be drawn from a maritime power, and how to make it the surest foundation of empire.

Pennies. I followed the plan, traced out by Themistocles, the ablest politician that Greece had ever produced. Nor did I begin the Peloponnesian War (as some have supposed) only to make myself necessary, and stop an inquiry into my public accounts. I really thought that the Republic of Athens could no longer defer a contest with Sparta, without giving up to that State the precedence in the direction of Greece and her own independence. To keep off for some time even a necessary war, with a probable hope of making it more advantageously at a favourable opportunity, is an act of true wisdom; but not to make it, when you see that your enemy will be strengthened, and your own advantages lost or considerably lessened, by the delay, is a most pernicious imprudence. With relation to my accounts, I had nothing to fear. I had not embezzled one drachma of public money, nor added one to my own paternal estate; and the people had placed so entire a confidence in me that they had allowed me, against the usual forms of their government, to dispose of large sums for secret service, without account. When, therefore, I advised the Peloponnesian War, I neither acted from private views, nor with the inconsiderate temerity of a restless ambition, but as became a wise statesman, who, having weighed all the dangers that may attend a great enterprise, and seeing a reasonable hope of good success, makes it his option to fight for dominion and glory, rather than sacrifice both to the uncertain possession of an insecure peace.

Cosmo. How were you sure of inducing so volatile a people to persevere in so steady a system of conduct as that which you had laid down, a system attended with much inconvenience and loss to particulars, while it presented but little to strike or inflame the imagination of the public? Bold and arduous enterprises, great battles, much bloodshed, and a speedy decision, are what the multitude desire in every war; but your plan of operation was the reverse of all this, and the execution of it required the temper of the Thebans rather than of the Athenians.

Pericles. I found, indeed, many symptoms of their impatience, but I was able to restrain it by the authority I had gained; for during my whole Ministry I never had stooped to court their favour by any unworthy means, never flattered them in their follies, nor complied with their passions against their true interests and my own better judgment; but used the power of my eloquence to keep them in the bounds of a wise moderation, to raise their spirits when too low, and show them their danger when they grew too presumptuous, the good effects of which conduct they had happily experienced in all their affairs. Whereas those who succeeded to me in the government, by their incapacity, their corruption, and their servile complaisance to the humour of the people, presently lost all the fruits of my virtue and prudence. Xerxes himself, I am convinced, did not suffer more by the flattery of his courtiers than the Athenians, after my decease, by that of their orators and Ministers of State.

Cosmo. Those orators could not gain the favour of the people by any other methods. Your arts were more noble, they were the arts of a statesman and of a prince. Your magnificent buildings (which in beauty of architecture surpassed any the world had ever seen), the statues of Phidias, the paintings of Zeuxis, the protection you gave to knowledge, genius, and abilities of every kind, added as much to the glory of Athens as to your popularity. And in this I may boast of an equal merit to Florence. For I embellished that city and the whole country about it with excellent buildings; I protected all arts; and, though I was not myself so eloquent or so learned as you, I no less encouraged those who were eminent in my time for their eloquence or their learning. Marcilius Ficinus, the second father of the Platonic philosophy, lived in my house, and conversed with me as intimately as Anaxagoras with you. Nor did I ever forget and suffer him so to want the necessaries of life as you did Anaxagoras, who had like to have perished by that unfriendly neglect; but to secure him at all times from any distress in his circumstances, and enable him to pursue his sublime speculations unmolested by low cares, I gave him an estate adjacent to one of my favourite villas. I also drew to Florence Argiropolo, the most learned Greek of those times, that, under my patronage, he might teach the Florentine youth the language and sciences of his country. But with regard to our buildings, there is this remarkable difference, yours were all raised at the expense of the public, mine at my own.

Pericles. My estate would bear no profuseness, nor allow me to exert the generosity of my nature. Your wealth exceeded that of any particular, or indeed of any prince who lived in your days. The vast commerce which, after the example of your ancestors, you continued to carry on in all parts of the world, even while you presided at the helm of the State, enabled you to do those splendid acts which rendered your name so illustrious. But I was constrained to make the public treasure the fund of my bounties; and I thought I could not possibly dispose of it better in time of peace than in finding employment for that part of the people which must else have been idle and useless to the community, introducing into Greece all the elegant arts, and adorning my country with works that are an honour to human nature; for, while I attended the most to these civil and peaceful occupations, I did not neglect to provide, with timely care, against war, nor suffer the nation to sink into luxury and effeminate softness. I kept our fleets in continual exercise, maintained a great number of seamen in constant pay, and disciplined well our land forces. Nor did I ever cease to recommend to all the Athenians, both by precepts and example, frugality, temperance, magnanimity, fortitude, and whatever could most effectually contribute to strengthen their bodies and minds.

Cosmo. Yet I have heard you condemned for rendering the people less sober and modest, by giving them a share of the conquered lands, and paying them wages for their necessary attendance in the public assemblies and other civil functions; but more especially for the vast and superfluous expense you entailed on the State in the theatrical spectacles with which you entertained them at the cost of the public.

Pericles. Perhaps I may have been too lavish in some of those bounties. Yet in a popular State it is necessary that the people should be amused, and should so far partake of the opulence of the public as not to suffer any want, which would render their minds too low and sordid for their political duties. In my time the revenues of Athens were sufficient to bear this charge; but afterwards, when we had lost the greatest part of our empire, it became, I must confess, too heavy a burden, and the continuance of it proved one cause of our ruin.

Cosmo. It is a most dangerous thing to load the State with largesses of that nature, or indeed with any unnecessary but popular charges, because to reduce them is almost impossible, though the circumstances of the public should necessarily demand a reduction. But did not you likewise, in order to advance your own greatness, throw into the hands of the people of Athens more power than the institutions of Solon had entrusted them with, and more than was consistent with the good of the State?

Pericles. We are now in the regions where Truth presides, and I dare not offend her by playing the orator in defence of my conduct. I must therefore acknowledge that, by weakening the power of the court of Areopagus, I tore up that anchor which Solon had wisely fixed to keep his Republic firm against the storms and fluctuations of popular factions. This alteration, which fundamentally injured the whole State, I made with a view to serve my own ambition, the only passion in my nature which I could not contain within the limits of virtue. For I knew that my eloquence would subject the people to me, and make them the willing instruments of all my desires; whereas the Areopagus had in it an authority and a dignity which I could not control. Thus by diminishing the counterpoise our Constitution had settled to moderate the excess of popular power, I augmented my own. But since my death I have been often reproached by the Shades of some of the most virtuous and wisest Athenians, who have fallen victims to the caprice or fury of the people, with having been the first cause of the injustice they suffered, and of all the mischiefs perpetually brought on my country by rash undertakings, bad conduct, and fluctuating councils. They say, I delivered up the State to the government of indiscreet or venal orators, and to the passions of a misguided, infatuated multitude, who thought their freedom consisted in encouraging calumnies against the best servants of the Commonwealth, and conferring power upon those who had no other merit than falling in with and soothing a popular folly. It is useless for me to plead that, during my life, none of these mischiefs were felt; that I employed my rhetoric to promote none but good and wise measures; that I was as free from any taint of avarice or corruption as Aristides himself. They reply that I am answerable for all the great evils occasioned afterwards by the want of that salutary restraint on the natural levity and extravagance of a democracy, which I had taken away. Socrates calls me the patron of Anytus, and Solon himself frowns upon me whenever we meet.

Cosmo. Solon has reason to do so; for tell me, Pericles, what opinion would you have of the architect you employed in your buildings if he had made them to last no longer than during the term of your life?

Pericles. The answer to your question will turn to your own condemnation. Your excessive liberalities to the indigent citizens, and the great sums you lent to all the noble families, did in reality buy the Republic of Florence, and gave your family such a power as enabled them to convert it from a popular State into an absolute monarchy.

Cosmo. The Florentines were so infested with discord and faction, and their commonwealth was so void of military virtue, that they could not have long been exempt from a more ignominious subjection to some foreign Power if those internal dissensions, with the confusion and anarchy they produced, had continued. But the Athenians had performed very glorious exploits, had obtained a great empire, and were become one of the noblest States in the world, before you altered the balance of their government. And after that alteration they declined very fast, till they lost all their greatness.

Pericles. Their constitution had originally a foul blemish in it, I mean, the ban of ostracism, which alone would have been sufficient to undo any State. For there is nothing of such important use to a nation as that men who most excel in wisdom and virtue should be encouraged to undertake the business of government. But this detestable custom deterred such men from serving the public, or, if they ventured to do so, turned even their own wisdom and virtue against them; so that in Athens it was safer to be infamous than renowned. We are told indeed, by the advocates for this strange institution, that it was not a punishment, but meant as a guard to the equality and liberty of the State; for which reason they deem it an honour done to the persons against whom it was used; as if words could change the real nature of things, and make a banishment of ten years, inflicted on a good citizen by the suffrages of his countrymen, no evil to him, or no offence against justice and the natural right every freeman may claim, that he shall not be expelled from any society of which he is a member without having first been proved guilty of some criminal action.

Cosmo. The ostracism was indeed a most unpardonable fault in the Athenian constitution. It placed envy in the seat of justice, and gave to private malice and public ingratitude a legal right to do wrong. Other nations are blamed for tolerating vice, but the Athenians alone would not tolerate virtue.

Pericles. The friends to the ostracism say that too eminent virtue destroys that equality which is the safeguard of freedom.

Cosmo. No State is well modelled if it cannot preserve itself from the danger of tyranny without a grievous violation of natural justice; nor would a friend to true freedom, which consists in being governed not by men but by laws, desire to live in a country where a Cleon bore rule, and where an Aristides was not suffered to remain. But, instead of remedying this evil, you made it worse. You rendered the people more intractable, more adverse to virtue, less subject to the laws, and more to impressions from mischievous demagogues, than they had been before your time.

Pericles. In truth, I did so; and therefore my place in Elysium, notwithstanding the integrity of my whole public conduct, and the great virtues I excited, is much below the rank of those who have governed commonwealths or limited monarchies, not merely with a concern for their present advantage, but also with a prudent regard to that balance of power on which their permanent happiness must necessarily depend.

DIALOGUE XXIV. LOCKE - BAYLE.

Bayle. Yes, we both were philosophers; but my philosophy was the deepest. You dogmatised; I doubted.

Locke. Do you make doubting a proof of depth in philosophy? It may be a good beginning of it, but it is a bad end.

Bayle. No; the more profound our searches are into the nature of things, the more uncertainty we shall find; and the most subtle minds see objections and difficulties in every system which are overlooked or undiscoverable by ordinary understandings.

Locke. It would be better, then, to be no philosopher, and to continue in the vulgar herd of mankind, that one may have the convenience of thinking that one knows something. I find that the eyes which Nature has given me see many things very clearly, though some are out of their reach, or discerned but dimly. What opinion ought I to have of a physician who should offer me an eye-water, the use of which would at first so sharpen my sight as to carry it farther than ordinary vision, but would in the end put them out? Your philosophy, Monsieur Bayle, is to the eyes of the mind what I have supposed the doctor's nostrum to be to those of the body. It actually brought your own excellent understanding, which was by nature quick-sighted, and rendered more so by art and a subtlety of logic peculiar to yourself, it brought, I say, your very acute understanding to see nothing clearly, and enveloped all the great truths of reason and religion in mists of doubt.

Bayle. I own it did; but your comparison is not just. I did not see well before I used my philosophic eye-water. I only supposed I saw well; but I was in an error, with all the rest of mankind. The blindness was real; the perceptions were imaginary. I cured myself first of those false imaginations, and then I laudably endeavoured to cure other men.

Locke. A great cure, indeed! and don't you think that, in return for the service you did them, they ought to erect you a statue?

Bayle. Yes; it is good for human nature to know its own weakness. When we arrogantly presume on a strength we have not, we are always in great danger of hurting ourselves or, at least, of deserving ridicule and contempt by vain and idle efforts.

Locke. I agree with you that human nature should know its own weakness; but it should also feel its strength, and try to improve it. This was my employment as a philosopher. I endeavoured to discover the real powers of the mind; to see what it could do, and what it could not; to restrain it from efforts beyond its ability, but to teach it how to advance as far as the faculties given to it by Nature, with the utmost exertion and most proper culture of them, would allow it to go. In the vast ocean of philosophy I had the line and the plummet always in my hands. Many of its depths I found myself unable to fathom; but by caution in sounding, and the careful observations I made in the course of my voyage, I found out some truths of so much use to mankind that they acknowledge me to have been their benefactor.

Bayle. Their ignorance makes them think so. Some other philosopher will come hereafter, and show those truths to be falsehoods. He will pretend to discover other truths of equal importance. A later sage will arise, perhaps among men now barbarous and unlearned, whose sagacious discoveries will discredit the opinions of his admired predecessor. In philosophy, as in Nature, all changes its form, and one thing exists by the destruction of another.

Locke. Opinions taken up without a patient investigation, depending on terms not accurately defined, and principles begged without proof, like theories to explain the phenomena of Nature built on suppositions instead of experiments, must perpetually change and destroy one another. But some opinions there are, even in matters not obvious to the common sense of mankind, which the mind has received on such rational grounds of assent that they are as immovable as the pillars of heaven, or (to speak philosophically) as the great laws of Nature, by which, under God, the universe is sustained. Can you seriously think that because the hypothesis of your countryman Descartes, which was nothing but an ingenious, well-imagined romance, has been lately exploded, the system of Newton, which is built on experiments and geometry, the two most certain methods of discovering truth, will ever fail? Or that, because the whims of fanatics and the divinity of the schoolmen cannot now be supported, the doctrines of that religion which I, the declared enemy of all enthusiasm and false reasoning, firmly believed and maintained, will ever be shaken?

Bayle. If you had asked Descartes, while he was in the height of his vogue, whether his system would be ever confuted by any other philosopher's, as that of Aristotle had been by his, what answer do you suppose he would have returned?

Locke. Come, come, Monsieur Bayle, you yourself know the difference between the foundations on which the credit of those systems and that of Newton is placed. Your scepticism is more affected than real. You found it a shorter way to a great reputation (the only wish of your heart) to object than to defend, to pull down than to set up. And your talents were admirable for that kind of work. Then your huddling together in a critical dictionary a pleasant tale, or obscene jest, and a grave argument against the Christian religion, a witty confutation of some absurd author, and an artful sophism to impeach some respectable truth, was particularly commodious to all our young smarts and smatterers in freethinking. But what mischief have you not done to human society! You have endeavoured, and with some degree of success, to shake those foundations on which the whole moral world and the great fabric of social happiness entirely rest. How could you, as a philosopher, in the sober hours of reflection, answer for this to your conscience, even supposing you had doubts of the truth of a system which gives to virtue its sweetest hopes, to impenitent vice its greatest fears, and to true penitence its best consolations; which restrains even the least approaches to guilt, and yet makes those allowances for the infirmities of our nature which the stoic pride denied to it, but which its real imperfection and the goodness of its infinitely benevolent Creator so evidently require?

Bayle. The mind is free, and it loves to exert its freedom. Any restraint upon it is a violence done to its nature, and a tyranny against which it has a right to rebel.

Locke. The mind, though free, has a governor within itself, which may and ought to limit the exercise of its freedom. That governor is reason.

Bayle. Yes; but reason, like other governors, has a policy more dependent upon uncertain caprice than upon any fixed laws. And if that reason which rules my mind or yours has happened to set up a favourite notion, it not only submits implicitly to it, but desires that the same respect should be paid to it by all the rest of mankind. Now I hold that any man may lawfully oppose this desire in another; and that if he is wise, he will do his utmost endeavours to check it in himself.

Locke. Is there not also a weakness of a contrary nature to this you are now ridiculing? Do we not often take a pleasure to show our own power and gratify our own pride by degrading notions set up by other men and generally respected?

Bayle. I believe we do; and by this means it often happens that if one man builds and consecrates a temple to folly, another pulls it down.

Locke. Do you think it beneficial to human society to have all temples pulled down?

Bayle. I cannot say that I do.

Locke. Yet I find not in your writings any mark of distinction to show us which you mean to save.

Bayle. A true philosopher, like an impartial historian, must be of no sect.

Locke. Is there no medium between the blind zeal of a sectary and a total indifference to all religion?

Bayle. With regard to morality I was not indifferent.

Locke. How could you, then, be indifferent with regard to the sanctions religion gives to morality? How could you publish what tends so directly and apparently to weaken in mankind the belief of those sanctions? Was not this sacrificing the great interests of virtue to the little motives of vanity?

Bayle. A man may act indiscreetly, but he cannot do wrong, by declaring that which, on a full discussion of the question, he sincerely thinks to be true.

Locke. An enthusiast who advances doctrines prejudicial to society, or opposes any that are useful to it, has the strength of opinion and the heat of a disturbed imagination to plead in alleviation of his fault; but your cool head and sound judgment can have no such excuse. I know very well there are passages in all your works, and those not a few, where you talk like a rigid moralist. I have also heard that your character was irreproachably good; but when, in the most laboured parts of your writings, you sap the surest foundations of all moral duties, what avails it that in others, or in the conduct of your life, you have appeared to respect them? How many who have stronger passions than you had, and are desirous to get rid of the curb that restrains them, will lay hold of your scepticism to set themselves loose from all obligations of virtue! What a misfortune is it to have made such a use of such talents! It would have been better for you and for mankind if you had been one of the dullest of Dutch theologians, or the most credulous monk in a Portuguese convent. The riches of the mind, like those of Fortune, may be employed so perversely as to become a nuisance and pest instead of an ornament and support to society.

Bayle. You are very severe upon me. But do you count it no merit, no service to mankind, to deliver them from the frauds and fetters of priestcraft, from the deliriums of fanaticism, and from the terrors and follies of superstition? Consider how much mischief these have done to the world! Even in the last age what massacres, what civil wars, what convulsions of government, what confusion in society, did they produce! Nay, in that we both lived in, though much more enlightened than the former, did I not see them occasion a violent persecution in my own country? And can you blame me for striking at the root of these evils.

Locke. The root of these evils, you well know, was false religion; but you struck at the true. Heaven and hell are not more different than the system of faith I defended and that which produced the horrors of which you speak. Why would you so fallaciously confound them together in some of your writings, that it requires much more judgment, and a more diligent attention than ordinary readers have, to separate them again, and to make the proper distinctions? This, indeed, is the great art of the most celebrated freethinkers. They recommend themselves to warm and ingenuous minds by lively strokes of wit, and by arguments really strong, against superstition, enthusiasm, and priestcraft; but at the same time they insidiously throw the colours of these upon the fair face of true religion, and dress her out in their garb, with a malignant intention to render her odious or despicable to those who have not penetration enough to discern the impious fraud. Some of them may have thus deceived themselves as well as others. Yet it is certain no book that ever was written by the most acute of these gentlemen is so repugnant to priestcraft, to spiritual tyranny, to all absurd superstitions, to all that can tend to disturb or injure society, as that Gospel they so much affect to despise.

Bayle. Mankind is so made that, when they have been over-heated, they cannot be brought to a proper temper again till they have been over-cooled. My scepticism might be necessary to abate the fever and frenzy of false religion.

Locke. A wise prescription, indeed, to bring on a paralytical state of the mind (for such a scepticism as yours is a palsy which deprives the mind of all vigour, and deadens its natural and vital powers) in order to take off a fever which temperance and the milk of the Evangelical doctrines would probably cure.

Bayle. I acknowledge that those medicines have a great power. But few doctors apply them untainted with the mixture of some harsher drugs or some unsafe and ridiculous nostrums of their own.

Locke. What you now say is too true. God has given us a most excellent physic for the soul in all its diseases, but bad and interested physicians, or ignorant and conceited quacks, administer it so ill to the rest of mankind that much of the benefit of it is unhappily lost.

DIALOGUE XXV. ARCHIBALD, EARL OF DOUGLAS, DUKE OF TOURAINE - JOHN, DUKE OF ARGYLE AND GREENWICH, FIELD-MARSHAL OF HIS BRITANNIC MAJESTY'S FORCES.

Argyle. Yes, noble Douglas, it grieves me that you and your son, together with the brave Earl of Buchan, should have employed so much valour and have thrown away your lives in fighting the battles of that State which, from its situation and interests, is the perpetual and most dangerous enemy to Great Britain. A British nobleman serving France appears to me as unfortunate and as much out of his proper sphere as a Grecian commander engaged in the service of Persia would have appeared to Aristides or Agesilaus.

Douglas. In serving France I served Scotland. The French were the natural allies to the Scotch, and by supporting their Crown I enabled my countrymen to maintain their independence against the English.

Argyle. The French, indeed, from the unhappy state of our country, were ancient allies to the Scotch, but that they ever were our natural allies I deny. Their alliance was proper and necessary for us, because we were then in an unnatural state, disunited from England. While that disunion continued, our monarchy was compelled to lean upon France for assistance and support. The French power and policy kept us, I acknowledge, independent of the English, but dependent on them; and this dependence exposed us to many grievous calamities by drawing on our country the formidable arms of the English whenever it happened that the French and they had a quarrel. The succours they afforded us were distant and uncertain. Our enemy was at hand, superior to us in strength, though not in valour. Our borders were ravaged; our kings were slain or led captive; we lost all the advantage of being the inhabitants of a great island; we had no commerce, no peace, no security, no degree of maritime power. Scotland was a back-door through which the French, with our help, made their inroads into England; if they conquered, we obtained little benefit from it; but if they were defeated, we were always the devoted victims on whom the conquerors severely wreaked their resentment.

Douglas. The English suffered as much in those wars as we. How terribly were their borders laid waste and depopulated by our sharp incursions! How often have the swords of my ancestors been stained with the best blood of that nation! Were not our victories at Bannockburn and at Otterburn as glorious as any that, with all the advantage of numbers, they have ever obtained over us?

Argyle. They were; but yet they did us no lasting good. They left us still dependent on the protection of France. They left us a poor, a feeble, a distressed, though a most valiant nation. They irritated England, but could not subdue it, nor hinder our feeling such effects of its enmity as gave us no reason to rejoice in our triumphs. How much more happily, in the auspicious reign of that queen who formed the Union, was my sword employed in humbling the foes of Great Britain! With how superior a dignity did I appear in the combined British senate, maintaining the interests of the whole united people of England and Scotland against all foreign powers who attempted to disturb our general happiness or to invade our common rights!

Douglas. Your eloquence and your valour had unquestionably a much nobler and more spacious field to exercise themselves in than any of those who defended the interests of only a part of the island.

Argyle. Whenever I read any account of the wars between the Scotch and the English, I think I am reading a melancholy history of civil dissensions. Whichever side is defeated, their loss appears to me a loss to the whole and an advantage to some foreign enemy of Great Britain. But the strength of that island is made complete by the Union, and what a great English poet has justly said in one instance is now true in all:

"The Hotspur and the Douglas, both together,   Are confident against the world in arms."

Who can resist the English and Scotch valour combined? When separated and opposed, they balanced each other; united, they will hold the balance of Europe. If all the Scotch blood that has been shed for the French in unnatural wars against England had been poured out to oppose the ambition of France, in conjunction with the English, if all the English blood that has been spilt as unfortunately in useless wars against Scotland had been preserved, France would long ago have been rendered incapable of disturbing our peace, and Great Britain would have been the most powerful of nations.

Douglas. There is truth in all you have said. But yet when I reflect on the insidious ambition of King Edward I., on the ungenerous arts he so treacherously employed to gain, or rather to steal, the sovereignty of our kingdom, and the detestable cruelty he showed to Wallace, our brave champion and martyr, my soul is up in arms against the insolence of the English, and I adore the memory of those patriots who died in asserting the independence of our Crown and the liberty of our nation.

Argyle. Had I lived in those days I should have joined with those patriots, and been the foremost to maintain so noble a cause. The Scotch were not made to be subject to the English. Their souls are too great for such a timid submission. But they may unite and incorporate with a nation they would not obey. Their scorn of a foreign yoke, their strong and generous love of independence and freedom, make their union with England more natural and more proper. Had the spirit of the Scotch been servile or base, it could never have coalesced with that of the English.

Douglas. It is true that the minds of both nations are congenial and filled with the same noble virtues, the same impatience of servitude, the same magnanimity, courage, and prudence, the same genius for policy, for navigation and commerce, for sciences and arts. Yet, notwithstanding this happy conformity, when I consider how long they were enemies to each other, what an hereditary hatred and jealousy had subsisted for many ages between them, what private passions, what prejudices, what contrary interests must have necessarily obstructed every step of the treaty, and how hard it was to overcome the strong opposition of national pride, I stand astonished that it was possible to unite the two kingdoms upon any conditions, and much more that it could be done with such equal regard and amicable fairness to both.

Argyle. It was indeed a most arduous and difficult undertaking. The success of it must, I think, be thankfully ascribed, not only to the great firmness and prudence of those who had the management of it, but to the gracious assistance of Providence for the preservation of the reformed religion amongst us, which, in that conjuncture, if the union had not been made, would have been ruined in Scotland and much endangered in England. The same good Providence has watched over and protected it since, in a most signal manner, against the attempts of an infatuated party in Scotland and the arts of France, who by her emissaries laboured to destroy it as soon as formed; because she justly foresaw that the continuance of it would be destructive to all her vast designs against the liberty of Europe. I myself had the honour to have a principal share in subduing one rebellion designed to subvert it, and since my death it has been, I hope, established for ever, not only by the defeat of another rebellion, which came upon us in the midst of a dangerous war with France, but by measures prudently taken in order to prevent such disturbances for the future. The ministers of the Crown have proposed and the British legislature has enacted a wise system of laws, the object of which is to reform and to civilise the Highlands of Scotland; to deliver the people there from the arbitrary power and oppression of their chieftains; to carry the royal justice and royal protection into the wildest parts of their mountains; to hinder their natural valour from being abused and perverted to the detriment of their country; and to introduce among them arts, agriculture, commerce, tranquillity, with all the improvements of social and polished life.

Douglas. By what you now tell me you give me the highest idea of the great prince, your master, who, after having been provoked by such a wicked rebellion, instead of enslaving the people of the Highlands, or laying the hand of power more heavily upon them (which is the usual consequence of unsuccessful revolts), has conferred on them the inestimable blessings of liberty, justice, and good order. To act thus is indeed to perfect the union and make all the inhabitants of Great Britain acknowledge, with gratitude and with joy, that they are subjects of the same well-regulated kingdom, and governed with the same impartial affection by the sovereign and father of the whole commonwealth.

Argyle. The laws I have mentioned and the humane benevolent policy of His Majesty's Government have already produced very salutary effects in that part of the kingdom, and, if steadily pursued, will produce many more. But no words can recount to you the infinite benefits which have attended the union in the northern counties of England and the southern of Scotland.

Douglas. The fruits of it must be, doubtless, most sensible there, where the perpetual enmity between the two nations had occasioned the greatest disorder and desolation.

Argyle. Oh, Douglas, could you revive and return into Scotland what a delightful alteration would you see in that country. All those great tracts of land, which in your time lay untilled on account of the inroads of the bordering English, or the feuds and discords that raged with perpetual violence within our own distracted kingdom, you would now behold cultivated and smiling with plenty. Instead of the castles, which every baron was compelled to erect for the defence of his family, and where he lived in the barbarism of Gothic pride, among miserable vassals oppressed by the abuse of his feudal powers, your eyes would be charmed with elegant country houses, adorned with fine plantations and beautiful gardens, while happy villages or gay towns are rising about them and enlivening the prospect with every image of rural wealth. On our coasts trading cities, full of new manufactures, and continually increasing the extent of their commerce. In our ports and harbours innumerable merchant ships, richly loaded, and protected from all enemies by the matchless fleet of Great Britain. But of all improvements the greatest is in the minds of the Scotch. These have profited, even more than their lands, by the culture which the settled peace and tranquillity produced by the union have happily given to them, and they have discovered such talents in all branches of literature as might render the English jealous of being excelled by their genius, if there could remain a competition, when there remains no distinction between the two nations.

Douglas. There may be emulation without jealousy, and the efforts, which that emulation will excite, may render our island superior in the fame of wit and good learning to Italy or to Greece; a superiority, which I have learnt in the Elysian fields to prefer even to that which is acquired by arms. But one doubt still remains with me concerning the union. I have been informed that no more than sixteen of our peers, except those who have English peerages (which some of the noblest have not), now sit in the House of Lords as representatives of the rest. Does not this in a great measure diminish those peers who are not elected? And have you not found the election of the sixteen too dependent on the favour of a court?

Argyle. It was impossible that the English could ever consent in the Treaty of Union, to admit a greater number to have places and votes in the Upper House of Parliament, but all the Scotch peerage is virtually there by representation. And those who are not elected have every dignity and right of the peerage, except the privilege of sitting in the House of Lords and some others depending thereon.

Douglas. They have so; but when parliaments enjoy such a share in the government of a country as ours do at this time, to be personally there is a privilege and a dignity of the highest importance.

Argyle. I wish it had been possible to impart it to all. But your reason will tell you it was not. And consider, my lord, that, till the Revolution in 1688, the power vested by our Government in the Lords of the Articles had made our parliaments much more subject to the influence of the Crown than our elections are now. As, by the manner in which they were constituted, those lords were no less devoted to the king than his own privy council, and as no proposition could then be presented in Parliament if rejected by them, they gave him a negative before debate. This, indeed, was abolished upon the accession of King William III., with many other oppressive and despotical powers, which had rendered our nobles abject slaves to the Crown, while they were allowed to be tyrants over the people. But if King James or his son had been restored, the government he had exercised would have been re-established, and nothing but the union of the two kingdoms could have effectually prevented that restoration. We likewise owe to the union the subsequent abolition of the Scotch privy council, which had been the most grievous engine of tyranny, and that salutary law which declared that no crimes should be high treason or misprision of treason in Scotland but such as were so in England, and gave us the English methods of trial in cases of that nature; whereas before there were so many species of treasons, the construction of them was so uncertain, and the trials were so arbitrary, that no man could be safe from suffering as a traitor. By the same Act of Parliament we also received a communication of that noble privilege of the English, exemption from torture, a privilege which, though essential both to humanity and to justice, no other nation in Europe, not even the freest republics, can boast of possessing. Shall we, then, take offence at some inevitable circumstances, which may be objected to, on our part, in the Treaty of Union, when it has delivered us from slavery, and all the worst evils that a state can suffer? It might be easily shown that, in his political and civil condition, every baron in Scotland is much happier now, and much more independent, than the highest was under that constitution of government which continued in Scotland even after the expulsion of King James II. The greatest enemies to the union are the friends of that king in whose reign, and in his brother's, the kingdom of Scotland was subjected to a despotism as arbitrary as that of France, and more tyrannically administered.

Douglas. All I have heard of those reigns makes me blush with indignation at the servility of our nobles, who could endure them so long. What, then, was become of that undaunted Scotch spirit, which had dared to resist the Plantagenets in the height of their power and pride? Could the descendants of those who had disdained to be subjects of Edward I. submit to be slaves of Charles II. or James?

Argyle. They seemed in general to have lost every characteristic of their natural temper, except a desire to abuse the royal authority for the gratification of their private resentments in family quarrels.

Douglas. Your grandfather, my lord, has the glory of not deserving this censure.

Argyle. I am proud that his spirit, and the principles he professed, drew upon him the injustice and fury of those times. But there needs no other proof than the nature and the manner of his condemnation to show what a wretched state our nobility then were in, and what an inestimable advantage it is to them that they are now to be tried as peers of Great Britain, and have the benefit of those laws which imparted to us the equity and the freedom of the English Constitution.

Upon the whole, as much as wealth is preferable to poverty, liberty to oppression, and national strength to national weakness, so much has Scotland incontestably gained by the union. England, too, has secured by it every public blessing which was before enjoyed by her, and has greatly augmented her strength. The martial spirit of the Scotch, their hardy bodies, their acute and vigorous minds, their industry, their activity, are now employed to the benefit of the whole island. He is now a bad Scotchman who is not a good Englishman, and he is a bad Englishman who is not a good Scotchman. Mutual intercourse, mutual interests, mutual benefits, must naturally be productive of mutual affection. And when that is established, when our hearts are sincerely united, many great things, which some remains of jealousy and distrust, or narrow local partialities, may hitherto have obstructed, will be done for the good of the whole United Kingdom. How much may the revenues of Great Britain be increased by the further increase of population, of industry, and of commerce in Scotland! What a mighty addition to the stock of national wealth will arise from the improvement of our most northern counties, which are infinitely capable of being improved! The briars and thorns are in a great measure grubbed up; the flowers and fruits may soon be planted. And what more pleasing, or what more glorious employment can any government have, than to attend to the cultivating of such a plantation?

Douglas. The prospect you open to me of happiness to my country appears so fair, that it makes me amends for the pain with which I reflect on the times wherein I lived, and indeed on our whole history for several ages.

Argyle. That history does, in truth, present to the mind a long series of the most direful objects, assassinations, rebellions, anarchy, tyranny, and religion itself, either cruel, or gloomy and unsocial. An historian who would paint it in its true colours must take the pencil of Guercino or Salvator Rosa. But the most agreeable imagination can hardly figure to itself a more pleasing scene of private and public felicity than will naturally result from the union, if all the prejudices against it, and all distinctions that may tend on either side to keep up an idea of separate interests, or to revive a sharp remembrance of national animosities, can be removed.

Douglas. If they can be removed! I think it impossible they can be retained. To resist the union is indeed to rebel against Nature. She has joined the two countries, has fenced them both with the sea against the invasion of all other nations, but has laid them entirely open the one to the other. Accursed be he who endeavours to divide them. What God has joined let no man put asunder.

DIALOGUE XXVI. CADMUS - HERCULES.

Hercules. Do you pretend to sit as high on Olympus as Hercules? Did you kill the Nemean lion, the Erymanthian boar, the Lernean serpent, and Stymphalian birds? Did you destroy tyrants and robbers? You value yourself greatly on subduing one serpent; I did as much as that while I lay in my cradle.

Cadmus. It is not on account of the serpent I boast myself a greater benefactor to Greece than you. Actions should be valued by their utility rather than their eclat. I taught Greece the art of writing, to which laws owe their precision and permanency. You subdued monsters; I civilised men. It is from untamed passions, not from wild beasts, that the greatest evils arise to human society. By wisdom, by art, by the united strength of civil community, men have been enabled to subdue the whole race of lions, bears, and serpents, and what is more, to bind in laws and wholesome regulations the ferocious violence and dangerous treachery of the human disposition. Had lions been destroyed only in single combat, men had had but a bad time of it; and what but laws could awe the men who killed the lions? The genuine glory, the proper distinction of the rational species, arises from the perfection of the mental powers. Courage is apt to be fierce, and strength is often exerted in acts of oppression. But wisdom is the associate of justice. It assists her to form equal laws, to pursue right measures, to correct power, protect weakness, and to unite individuals in a common interest and general welfare. Heroes may kill tyrants, but it is wisdom and laws that prevent tyranny and oppression. The operations of policy far surpass the labours of Hercules, preventing many evils which valour and might cannot even redress. You heroes consider nothing but glory, and hardly regard whether the conquests which raise your fame are really beneficial to your country. Unhappy are the people who are governed by valour not directed by prudence, and not mitigated by the gentle arts!

Hercules. I do not expect to find an admirer of my strenuous life in the man who taught his countrymen to sit still and read, and to lose the hours of youth and action in idle speculation and the sport of words.

Cadmus. An ambition to have a place in the registers of fame is the Eurystheus which imposes heroic labours on mankind. The muses incite to action as well as entertain the hours of repose; and I think you should honour them for presenting to heroes such a noble recreation as may prevent their taking up the distaff when they lay down the club.

Hercules. Wits as well as heroes can take up the distaff. What think you of their thin-spun systems of philosophy, or lascivious poems, or Milesian fables? Nay, what is still worse, are there not panegyrics on tyrants, and books that blaspheme the gods and perplex the natural sense of right and wrong? I believe if Eurystheus was to set me to work again he would find me a worse task than any he imposed; he would make me read through a great library; and I would serve it as I did the hydra, I would burn as I went on, that one chimera might not rise from another to plague mankind. I should have valued myself more on clearing the library than on cleansing the Augean stables.

Cadmus. It is in those libraries only that the memory of your labours exists. The heroes of Marathon, the patriots of Thermopylae, owe their immortality to me. All the wise institutions of lawgivers and all the doctrines of sages had perished in the ear, like a dream related, if letters had not preserved them. Oh Hercules! it is not for the man who preferred virtue to pleasure to be an enemy to the muses. Let Sardanapalus and the silken sons of luxury, who have wasted life in inglorious ease, despise the records of action which bear no honourable testimony to their lives. But true merit, heroic virtue, each genuine offspring of immortal Jove, should honour the sacred source of lasting fame.

Hercules. Indeed, if writers employed themselves only in recording the acts of great men, much might be said in their favour. But why do they trouble people with their meditations? Can it signify to the world what an idle man has been thinking?

Cadmus. Yes, it may. The most important and extensive advantages mankind enjoy are greatly owing to men who have never quitted their closets. To them mankind is obliged for the facility and security of navigation. The invention of the compass has opened to them new worlds. The knowledge of the mechanical powers has enabled them to construct such wonderful machines as perform what the united labour of millions by the severest drudgery could not accomplish. Agriculture, too, the most useful of arts, has received its share of improvement from the same source. Poetry likewise is of excellent use to enable the memory to retain with more ease, and to imprint with more energy upon the heart, precepts of virtue and virtuous actions. Since we left the world, from the little root of a few letters, science has spread its branches over all nature, and raised its head to the heavens. Some philosophers have entered so far into the counsels of divine wisdom as to explain much of the great operations of nature. The dimensions and distances of the planets, the causes of their revolutions, the path of comets, and the ebbing and flowing of tides are understood and explained. Can anything raise the glory of the human species more than to see a little creature, inhabiting a small spot, amidst innumerable worlds, taking a survey of the universe, comprehending its arrangement, and entering into the scheme of that wonderful connection and correspondence of things so remote, and which it seems the utmost exertion of Omnipotence to have established? What a volume of wisdom, what a noble theology do these discoveries open to us! While some superior geniuses have soared to these sublime subjects, other sagacious and diligent minds have been inquiring into the most minute works of the Infinite Artificer; the same care, the same providence is exerted through the whole, and we should learn from it that to true wisdom utility and fitness appear perfection, and whatever is beneficial is noble.

Hercules. I approve of science as far as it is assistant to action. I like the improvement of navigation and the discovery of the greater part of the globe, because it opens a wider field for the master spirits of the world to bustle in.

Cadmus. There spoke the soul of Hercules. But if learned men are to be esteemed for the assistance they give to active minds in their schemes, they are not less to be valued for their endeavours to give them a right direction and moderate their too great ardour. The study of history will teach the warrior and the legislator by what means armies have been victorious and states have become powerful; and in the private citizen they will inculcate the love of liberty and order. The writings of sages point out a private path of virtue, and show that the best empire is self-government, and subduing our passions the noblest of conquests.

Hercules. The true spirit of heroism acts by a sort of inspiration, and wants neither the experience of history nor the doctrines of philosophers to direct it. But do not arts and sciences render men effeminate, luxurious, and inactive? and can you deny that wit and learning are often made subservient to very bad purposes?

Cadmus. I will own that there are some natures so happily formed they hardly want the assistance of a master, and the rules of art, to give them force or grace in everything they do. But these heaven-inspired geniuses are few. As learning flourishes only where ease, plenty, and mild government subsist, in so rich a soil, and under so soft a climate, the weeds of luxury will spring up among the flowers of art; but the spontaneous weeds would grow more rank, if they were allowed the undisturbed possession of the field. Letters keep a frugal, temperate nation from growing ferocious, a rich one from becoming entirely sensual and debauched. Every gift of the gods is sometimes abused; but wit and fine talents by a natural law gravitate towards virtue; accidents may drive them out of their proper direction; but such accidents are a sort of prodigies, and, like other prodigies, it is an alarming omen, and of dire portent to the times. For if virtue cannot keep to her allegiance those men, who in their hearts confess her divine right, and know the value of her laws, on whose fidelity and obedience can she depend? May such geniuses never descend to flatter vice, encourage folly, or propagate irreligion; but exert all their powers in the service of virtue, and celebrate the noble choice of those, who, like you, preferred her to pleasure.

DIALOGUE XXVII. MERCURY - AND A MODERN FINE LADY.

Mrs. Modish. Indeed, Mr. Mercury, I cannot have the pleasure of waiting upon you now. I am engaged, absolutely engaged.

Mercury. I know you have an amiable, affectionate husband, and several fine children; but you need not be told, that neither conjugal attachments, maternal affections, nor even the care of a kingdom's welfare or a nation's glory, can excuse a person who has received a summons to the realms of death. If the grim messenger was not as peremptory as unwelcome, Charon would not get a passenger (except now and then a hypochondriacal Englishman) once in a century. You must be content to leave your husband and family, and pass the Styx.

Mrs. Modish. I did not mean to insist on any engagement with my husband and children; I never thought myself engaged to them. I had no engagements but such as were common to women of my rank. Look on my chimney-piece, and you will see I was engaged to the play on Mondays, balls on Tuesdays, the opera on Saturdays, and to card assemblies the rest of the week, for two months to come; and it would be the rudest thing in the world not to keep my appointments. If you will stay for me till the summer season, I will wait on you with all my heart. Perhaps the Elysian fields may be less detestable than the country in our world. Pray have you a fine Vauxhall and Ranelagh? I think I should not dislike drinking the Lethe waters when you have a full season.

Mercury. Surely you could not like to drink the waters of oblivion, who have made pleasure the business, end, and aim of your life! It is good to drown cares, but who would wash away the remembrance of a life of gaiety and pleasure.

Mrs. Modish. Diversion was indeed the business of my life, but as to pleasure, I have enjoyed none since the novelty of my amusements was gone off. Can one be pleased with seeing the same thing over and over again? Late hours and fatigue gave me the vapours, spoiled the natural cheerfulness of my temper, and even in youth wore away my youthful vivacity.

Mercury. If this way of life did not give you pleasure, why did you continue in it? I suppose you did not think it was very meritorious?

Mrs. Modish. I was too much engaged to think at all: so far indeed my manner of life was agreeable enough. My friends always told me diversions were necessary, and my doctor assured me dissipation was good for my spirits; my husband insisted that it was not, and you know that one loves to oblige one's friends, comply with one's doctor, and contradict one's husband; and besides I was ambitious to be thought du bon ton.

Mercury. Bon ton! what is that, madam? Pray define it.

Mrs. Modish. Oh sir, excuse me, it is one of the privileges of the bon ton never to define, or be defined. It is the child and the parent of jargon. It is, I can never tell you what it is: but I will try to tell you what it is not. In conversation it is not wit; in manners it is not politeness; in behaviour it is not address; but it is a little like them all. It can only belong to people of a certain rank, who live in a certain manner, with certain persons, who have not certain virtues, and who have certain vices, and who inhabit a certain part of the town. Like a place by courtesy, it gets a higher rank than the person can claim, but which those who have a legal title to precedency dare not dispute, for fear of being thought not to understand the rules of politeness. Now, sir, I have told you as much as I know of it, though I have admired and aimed at it all my life.

Mercury. Then, madam, you have wasted your time, faded your beauty, and destroyed your health, for the laudable purposes of contradicting your husband, and being this something and this nothing called the bon ton.

Mrs. Modish. What would you have had me do?

Mercury. I will follow your mode of instructing. I will tell you what I would not have had you do. I would not have had you sacrifice your time, your reason, and your duties, to fashion and folly. I would not have had you neglect your husband's happiness and your children's education.

Mrs. Modish. As to the education of my daughters, I spared no expense; they had a dancing-master, music-master, and drawing-mister, and a French governess to teach them behaviour and the French language.

Mercury. So their religion, sentiments, and manners were to be learnt from a dancing-master, music-master, and a chambermaid! Perhaps they might prepare them to catch the bon ton. Your daughters must have been so educated as to fit them to be wives without conjugal affection, and mothers without maternal care. I am sorry for the sort of life they are commencing, and for that which you have just concluded. Minos is a sour old gentleman, without the least smattering of the bon ton, and I am in a fright for you. The best thing I can advise you is to do in this world as you did in the other, keep happiness in your view, but never take the road that leads to it. Remain on this side Styx, wander about without end or aim, look into the Elysian fields, but never attempt to enter into them, lest Minos should push you into Tartarus; for duties neglected may bring on a sentence not much less severe than crimes committed.

DIALOGUE XXVIII. PLUTARCH – CHARON - AND A MODERN BOOKSELLER.

Charon. Here is a fellow who is very unwilling to land in our territories. He says he is rich, has a great deal of business in the other world, and must needs return to it; he is so troublesome and obstreperous I know not what to do with him. Take him under your care, therefore, good Plutarch; you will easily awe him into order and decency by the superiority an author has over a bookseller.

Bookseller. Am I got into a world so absolutely the reverse of that I left, that here authors domineer over booksellers? Dear Charon, let me go back, and I will pay any price for my passage; but, if I must stay, leave me not with any of those who are styled classical authors. As to you, Plutarch, I have a particular animosity against you for having almost occasioned my ruin. When I first set up shop, understanding but little of business, I unadvisedly bought an edition of your "Lives," a pack of old Greeks and Romans, which cost me a great sum of money. I could never get off above twenty sets of them. I sold a few to the Universities, and some to Eton and Westminster, for it is reckoned a pretty book for boys and undergraduates; but, unless a man has the luck to light on a pedant, he shall not sell a set of them in twenty years.

Plutarch. From the merit of the subjects, I had hoped another reception for my works. I will own, indeed, that I am not always perfectly accurate in every circumstance, nor do I give so exact and circumstantial a detail of the actions of my heroes as may be expected from a biographer who has confined himself to one or two characters. A zeal to preserve the memory of great men, and to extend the influence of such noble examples, made me undertake more than I could accomplish in the first degree of perfection; but surely the characters of my illustrious men are not so imperfectly sketched that they will not stand forth to all ages as patterns of virtue and incitements to glory. My reflections are allowed to be deep and sagacious; and what can be more useful to a reader than a wise man's judgment on a great man's conduct? In my writings you will find no rash censures, no undeserved encomiums, no mean compliance with popular opinions, no vain ostentation of critical skill, nor any affected finesse. In my "Parallels," which used to be admired as pieces of excellent judgment, I compare with perfect impartiality one great man with another, and each with the rule of justice. If, indeed, latter ages have produced greater men and better writers, my heroes and my works ought to give place to them. As the world has now the advantage of much better rules of morality than the unassisted reason of poor Pagans could form, I do not wonder that those vices, which appeared to us as mere blemishes in great characters, should seem most horrid deformities in the purer eyes of the present age, a delicacy I do not blame, but admire and commend. And I must censure you for endeavouring, if you could publish better examples, to obtrude on your countrymen such as were defective. I rejoice at the preference which they give to perfect and unalloyed virtue; and as I shall ever retain a high veneration for the illustrious men of every age, I should be glad if you would give me some account of those persons who in wisdom, justice, valour, patriotism, have eclipsed my Solon, Numa, Camillus, and other boasts of Greece or Rome.

Bookseller. Why, Master Plutarch, you are talking Greek indeed. That work which repaired the loss I sustained by the costly edition of your books was "The Lives of the Highwaymen;" but I should never have grown rich if it had not been by publishing "The Lives of Men that Never Lived." You must know that, though in all times it was possible to have a great deal of learning and very little wisdom, yet it is only by a modern improvement in the art of writing that a man may read all his life and have no learning or knowledge at all, which begins to be an advantage of the greatest importance. There is as natural a war between your men of science and fools as between the cranes and the pigmies of old. Most of our young men having deserted to the fools, the party of the learned is near being beaten out of the field; and I hope in a little while they will not dare to peep out of their forts and fastnesses at Oxford and Cambridge. There let them stay and study old musty moralists till one falls in love with the Greek, another with the Roman virtue; but our men of the world should read our new books, which teach them to have no virtue at all. No book is fit for a gentleman's reading which is not void of facts and of doctrines, that he may not grow a pedant in his morals or conversation. I look upon history (I mean real history) to be one of the worst kinds of study. Whatever has happened may happen again, and a well-bred man may unwarily mention a parallel instance he had met with in history and be betrayed into the awkwardness of introducing into his discourse a Greek, a Roman, or even a Gothic name; but when a gentleman has spent his time in reading adventures that never occurred, exploits that never were achieved, and events that not only never did, but never can happen, it is impossible that in life or in discourse he should ever apply them. A secret history, in which there is no secret and no history, cannot tempt indiscretion to blab or vanity to quote; and by this means modern conversation flows gentle and easy, unencumbered with matter and unburdened of instruction. As the present studies throw no weight or gravity into discourse and manners, the women are not afraid to read our books, which not only dispose to gallantry and coquetry, but give rules for them. Caesar's "Commentaries," and the "Account of Xenophon's Expedition," are not more studied by military commanders than our novels are by the fair, to a different purpose, indeed; for their military maxims teach to conquer, ours to yield. Those inflame the vain and idle love of glory: these inculcate a noble contempt of reputation. The women have greater obligations to our writers than the men. By the commerce of the world men might learn much of what they get from books; but the poor women, who in their early youth are confined and restrained, if it were not for the friendly assistance of books, would remain long in an insipid purity of mind, with a discouraging reserve of behaviour.

Plutarch. As to your men who have quitted the study of virtue for the study of vice, useful truth for absurd fancy, and real history for monstrous fiction, I have neither regard nor compassion for them; but I am concerned for the women who are betrayed into these dangerous studies; and I wish for their sakes I had expatiated more on the character of Lucretia and some other heroines.

Bookseller. I tell you, our women do not read in order to live or to die like Lucretia. If you would inform us that a billet-doux was found in her cabinet after her death, or give a hint as if Tarquin really saw her in the arms of a slave, and that she killed herself not to suffer the shame of a discovery, such anecdotes would sell very well. Or if, even by tradition, but better still, if by papers in the Portian family, you could show some probability that Portia died of dram drinking, you would oblige the world very much; for you must know, that next to new-invented characters, we are fond of new lights upon ancient characters; I mean such lights as show a reputed honest man to have been a concealed knave, an illustrious hero a pitiful coward, &c. Nay, we are so fond of these kinds of information as to be pleased sometimes to see a character cleared from a vice or crime it has been charged with, provided the person concerned be actually dead. But in this case the evidence must be authentic, and amount to a demonstration; in the other, a detection is not necessary; a slight suspicion will do, if it concerns a really good and great character.

Plutarch. I am the more surprised at what you say of the taste of your contemporaries, as I met with a Frenchman who assured me that less than a century ago he had written a much admired "Life of Cyrus," under the name of Artamenes, in which he ascribed to him far greater actions than those recorded of him by Xenophon and Herodotus; and that many of the great heroes of history had been treated in the same manner; that empires were gained and battles decided by the valour of a single man, imagination bestowing what nature has denied, and the system of human affairs rendered impossible.

Bookseller. I assure you those books were very useful to the authors and their booksellers; and for whose benefit besides should a man write? These romances were very fashionable and had a great sale: they fell in luckily with the humour of the age.

Plutarch. Monsieur Scuderi tells me they were written in the times of vigour and spirit, in the evening of the gallant days of chivalry, which, though then declining, had left in the hearts of men a warm glow of courage and heroism; and they were to be called to books as to battle, by the sound of the trumpet. He says, too, that if writers had not accommodated themselves to the prejudices of the age, and written of bloody battles and desperate encounters, their works would have been esteemed too effeminate an amusement for gentlemen. Histories of chivalry, instead of enervating, tend to invigorate the mind, and endeavour to raise human nature above the condition which is naturally prescribed to it; but as strict justice, patriotic motives, prudent counsels, and a dispassionate choice of what upon the whole is fittest and best, do not direct these heroes of romance, they cannot serve for instruction and example, like the great characters of true history. It has ever been my opinion, that only the clear and steady light of truth can guide men to virtue, and that the lesson which is impracticable must be unuseful. Whoever shall design to regulate his conduct by these visionary characters will be in the condition of superstitious people, who choose rather to act by intimations they receive in the dreams of the night, than by the sober counsels of morning meditation. Yet I confess it has been the practice of many nations to incite men to virtue by relating the deeds of fabulous heroes: but surely it is the custom only of yours to incite them to vice by the history of fabulous scoundrels. Men of fine imagination have soared into the regions of fancy to bring back Astrea; you go thither in search of Pandora. Oh disgrace to letters! Oh shame to the muses!

Bookseller. You express great indignation at our present race of writers; but believe me the fault lies chiefly on the side of the readers. As Monsieur Scuderi observed to you, authors must comply with the manners and disposition of those who are to read them. There must be a certain sympathy between the book and the reader to create a good liking. Would you present a modern fine gentleman, who is negligently lolling in an easy chair, with the labours of Hercules for his recreation? or make him climb the Alps with Hannibal when he is expiring with the fatigue of last night's ball? Our readers must be amused, flattered, soothed; such adventures must be offered to them as they would like to have a share in.

Plutarch. It should be the first object of writers to correct the vices and follies of the age. I will allow as much compliance with the mode of the times as will make truth and good morals agreeable. Your love of fictitious characters might be turned to good purpose if those presented to the public were to be formed on the rules of religion and morality. It must be confessed that history, being employed only about illustrious persons, public events, and celebrated actions, does not supply us with such instances of domestic merit as one could wish. Our heroes are great in the field and the senate, and act well in great scenes on the theatre of the world; but the idea of a man, who in the silent retired path of life never deviates into vice, who considers no spectator but the Omniscient Being, and solicits no applause but His approbation, is the noblest model that can be exhibited to mankind, and would be of the most general use. Examples of domestic virtue would be more particularly useful to women than those of great heroines. The virtues of women are blasted by the breath of public fame, as flowers that grow on an eminence are faded by the sun and wind which expand them. But true female praise, like the music of the spheres, arises from a gentle, a constant, and an equal progress in the path marked out for them by their great Creator; and, like the heavenly harmony, it is not adapted to the gross ear of mortals, but is reserved for the delight of higher beings, by whose wise laws they were ordained to give a silent light and shed a mild, benignant influence on the world.

Bookseller. We have had some English and French writers who aimed at what you suggest. In the supposed character of Clarissa (said a clergyman to me a few days before I left the world) one finds the dignity of heroism tempered by the meekness and humility of religion, a perfect purity of mind, and sanctity of manners. In that of Sir Charles Grandison, a noble pattern of every private virtue, with sentiments so exalted as to render him equal to every public duty.

Plutarch. Are both these characters by the same author?

Bookseller. Ay, Master Plutarch, and what will surprise you more, this author has printed for me.

Plutarch. By what you say, it is pity he should print any work but his own. Are there no other authors who write in this manner?

Bookseller. Yes, we have another writer of these imaginary histories; one who has not long since descended to these regions. His name is Fielding, and his works, as I have heard the best judges say, have a true spirit of comedy and an exact representation of nature, with fine moral touches. He has not, indeed, given lessons of pure and consummate virtue, but he has exposed vice and meanness with all the powers of ridicule; and we have some other good wits who have exerted their talents to the purposes you approve. Monsieur de Marivaux, and some other French writers, have also proceeded much upon the same plan with a spirit and elegance which give their works no mean rank among the belles lettres. I will own that, when there is wit and entertainment enough in a book to make it sell, it is not the worse for good morals.

Charon. I think, Plutarch, you have made this gentleman a little more humble, and now I will carry him the rest of his journey. But he is too frivolous an animal to present to wise Minos. I wish Mercury were here; he would damn him for his dulness. I have a good mind to carry him to the Danaides, and leave him to pour water into their vessels which, like his late readers, are destined to eternal emptiness. Or shall I chain him to the rock, side to side by Prometheus, not for having attempted to steal celestial fire, in order to animate human forms, but for having endeavoured to extinguish that which Jupiter had imparted? Or shall we constitute him friseur to Tisiphone, and make him curl up her locks with his satires and libels?

Plutarch. Minos does not esteem anything frivolous that affects the morals of mankind. He punishes authors as guilty of every fault they have countenanced and every crime they have encouraged, and denounces heavy vengeance for the injuries which virtue or the virtuous have suffered in consequence of their writings.

DIALOGUE XXIX. PUBLIUS CORNELIUS SCIPIO AFRICANUS - CAIUS JULIUS CAESAR.

Scipio. Alas, Caesar! how unhappily did you end a life made illustrious by the greatest exploits in war and most various civil talents!

Caesar. Can Scipio wonder at the ingratitude of Rome to her generals? Did not he reproach her with it in the epitaph he ordered to be inscribed upon his tomb at Liternum, that mean village in Campania, to which she had driven the conqueror of Hannibal and of Carthage? I also, after subduing her most dangerous enemies, the Helvetians, the Gauls, and the Germans, after raising her name to the highest pitch of glory, should have been deprived of my province, reduced to live as a private man under the power of my enemies and the enviers of my greatness; nay, brought to a trial and condemned by the judgment of a faction, if I had not led my victorious troops to Rome, and by their assistance, after all my offers of peace had been iniquitously rejected, made myself master of a State which knew so ill how to recompense superior merit. Resentment of this, together with the secret machinations of envy, produced not long afterwards a conspiracy of senators, and even of some whom I had most obliged and loved, against my life, which they basely took away by assassination.

Scipio. You say you led your victorious troops to Rome. How were they your troops? I thought the Roman armies had belonged to the Republic, not to their generals.

Caesar. They did so in your time. But before I came to command them, Marius and Sylla had taught them that they belonged to their generals. And I taught the senate that a veteran army, affectionately attached to its leader, could give him all the treasures and honours of the State without asking their leave.

Scipio. Just gods! did I then deliver my country from the invading Carthaginian, did I exalt it by my victories above all other nations, that it might become a richer prey to its own rebel soldiers and their ambitious commanders?

Caesar. How could it be otherwise? Was it possible that the conquerors of Europe, Asia, and Africa could tamely submit to descend from their triumphal chariots and become subject to the authority of praetors and consuls elected by a populace corrupted by bribes, or enslaved to a confederacy of factious nobles, who, without regard to merit, considered all the offices and dignities of the State as hereditary possessions belonging to their families?

Scipio. If I thought it no dishonour, after triumphing over Hannibal, to lay down my fasces and obey, as all my ancestors had done before me, the magistrates of the republic, such a conduct would not have dishonoured either Marius, or Sylla, or Caesar. But you all dishonoured yourselves when, instead of virtuous Romans, superior to your fellow-citizens in merit and glory, but equal to them in a due subjection to the laws, you became the enemies, the invaders, and the tyrants of your country.

Caesar. Was I the enemy of my country in giving it a ruler fit to support all the majesty and weight of its empire? Did I invade it when I marched to deliver the people from the usurped dominion and insolence of a few senators? Was I a tyrant because I would not crouch under Pompey, and let him be thought my superior when I felt he was not my equal?

Scipio. Pompey had given you a noble example of moderation in twice dismissing the armies, at the head of which he had performed such illustrious actions, and returning a private citizen into the bosom of his country.

Caesar. His moderation was a cheat. He believed that the authority his victories had gained him would make him effectually master of the commonwealth without the help of those armies. But finding it difficult to subdue the united opposition of Crassus and me, he leagued himself with us, and in consequence of that league we three governed the empire. But, after the death of Crassus, my glorious achievements in subduing the Gauls raised such a jealousy in him that he could no longer endure me as a partner in his power, nor could I submit to degrade myself into his subject.

Scipio. Am I then to understand that the civil war you engaged in was really a mere contest whether you or Pompey should remain sole lord of Rome?

Caesar. Not so, for I offered, in my letters to the senate, to lay down my arms if Pompey at the same time would lay down his, and leave the republic in freedom. Nor did I resolve to draw the sword till not only the senate, overpowered by the fear of Pompey and his troops, had rejected these offers, but two tribunes of the people, for legally and justly interposing their authority in my behalf, had been forced to fly from Rome disguised in the habit of slaves, and take refuge in my camp for the safety of their persons. My camp was therefore the asylum of persecuted liberty, and my army fought to avenge the violation of the rights and majesty of the people as much as to defend the dignity of their general unjustly oppressed.

Scipio. You would therefore have me think that you contended for the equality and liberty of the Romans against the tyranny of Pompey and his lawless adherents. In such a war I, myself, if I had lived in your times, would have willingly been your lieutenant. Tell me then, on the issue of this honourable enterprise, when you had subdued all your foes and had no opposition remaining to obstruct your intentions, did you establish that liberty for which you fought? Did you restore the republic to what it was in my time?

Caesar. I took the necessary measures to secure to myself the fruits of my victories, and gave a head to the empire, which could neither subsist without one nor find another so well suited to the greatness of the body.

Scipio. There the true character of Caesar was seen unmasked. You had managed so skilfully in the measures which preceded the civil war, your offers were so specious, and there appeared so much violence in the conduct of your enemies that, if you had fallen in that war, posterity might have doubted whether you were not a victim to the interests of your country. But your success, and the despotism you afterwards exorcised, took off those disguises and showed clearly that the aim of all your actions was tyranny.

Caesar. Let us not deceive ourselves with sounds and names. That great minds should aspire to sovereign power is a fixed law of Nature. It is an injury to mankind if the highest abilities are not placed in the highest stations. Had you, Scipio, been kept down by the republican jealousy of Cato, the censor Hannibal would have never been recalled out of Italy nor defeated in Africa. And if I had not been treacherously murdered by the daggers of Brutus and Cassius, my sword would have avenged the defeat of Crassus and added the empire of Parthia to that of Rome. Nor was my government tyrannical. It was mild, humane, and bounteous. The world would have been happy under it and wished its continuance, but my death broke the pillars of the public tranquillity and brought upon the whole empire a direful scene of calamity and confusion.

Scipio. You say that great minds will naturally aspire to sovereign power. But, if they are good as well as great, they will regulate their ambition by the laws of their country. The laws of Rome permitted me to aspire to the conduct of the war against Carthage; but they did not permit you to turn her arms against herself, and subject her to your will. The breach of one law of liberty is a greater evil to a nation than the loss of a province; and, in my opinion, the conquest of the whole world would not be enough to compensate for the total loss of their freedom.

Caesar. You talk finely, Africanus; but ask yourself, whether the height and dignity of your mind, that noble pride which accompanies the magnanimity of a hero, could always stoop to a nice conformity with the laws of your country? Is there a law of liberty more essential, more sacred, than that which obliges every member of a free community to submit himself to a trial, upon a legal charge brought against him for a public misdemeanour? In what manner did you answer a regular accusation from a tribune of the people, who charged you with embezzling the money of the State? You told your judges that on that day you had vanquished Hannibal and Carthage, and bade them follow you to the temples to give thanks to the gods. Nor could you ever be brought to stand a legal trial, or justify those accounts, which you had torn in the senate when they were questioned there by two magistrates in the name of the Roman people. Was this acting like the subject of a free State? Had your victory procured you an exemption from justice? Had it given into your hands the money of the republic without account? If it had, you were king of Rome. Pharsalia, Thapsus, and Munda could do no more for me.

Scipio. I did not question the right of bringing me to a trial, but I disdained to plead in vindication of a character so unspotted as mine. My whole life had been an answer to that infamous charge.

Caesar. It may be so; and, for my part, I admire the magnanimity of your behaviour. But I should condemn it as repugnant and destructive to liberty, if I did not pay more respect to the dignity of a great general, than to the forms of a democracy or the rights of a tribune.

Scipio. You are endeavouring to confound my cause with yours; but they are exceedingly different. You apprehended a sentence of condemnation against you for some part of your conduct, and, to prevent it, made an impious war on your country, and reduced her to servitude. I trusted the justification of my affronted innocence to the opinion of my judges, scorning to plead for myself against a charge unsupported by any other proof than bare suspicions and surmises. But I made no resistance; I kindled no civil war; I left Rome undisturbed in the enjoyment of her liberty. Had the malice of my accusers been ever so violent, had it threatened my destruction, I should have chosen much rather to turn my sword against my own bosom than against that of my country.

Caesar. You beg the question in supposing that I really hurt my country by giving her a master. When Cato advised the senate to make Pompey sole consul, he did it upon this principle, that any kind of government is preferable to anarchy. The truth of this, I presume, no man of sense will contest; and the anarchy, which that zealous defender of liberty so much apprehended, would have continued in Rome, if that power, which the urgent necessity of the State conferred upon me, had not removed it.

Scipio. Pompey and you had brought that anarchy on the State in order to serve your own ends. It was owing to the corruption, the factions, and the violence which you had encouraged from an opinion that the senate would be forced to submit to an absolute power in your hands, as a remedy against those intolerable evils. But Cato judged well in thinking it eligible to make Pompey sole consul rather than you dictator, because experience had shown that Pompey respected the forms of the Roman constitution; and though he sought, by bad means as well as good, to obtain the highest magistracies and the most honourable commands, yet he laid them down again, and contented himself with remaining superior in credit to any other citizen.

Caesar. If all the difference between my ambition and Pompey's was only, as you represent it, in a greater or less respect for the forms of the constitution, I think it was hardly becoming such a patriot as Cato to take part in our quarrel, much less to kill himself rather than yield to my power.

Scipio. It is easier to revive the spirit of liberty in a government where the forms of it remain unchanged, than where they have been totally disregarded and abolished. But I readily own that the balance of the Roman constitution had been destroyed by the excessive and illegal authority which the people were induced to confer upon Pompey, before any extraordinary honours or commands had been demanded by you. And that is, I think, your best excuse.

Caesar. Yes, surely. The favourers of the Manilian law had an ill grace in desiring to limit the commissions I obtained from the people, according to the rigour of certain absolute republican laws, no more regarded in my time than the Sybilline oracles or the pious institutions of Numa.

Scipio. It was the misfortune of your time that they were not regarded. A virtuous man would not take from a deluded people such favours as they ought not to bestow. I have a right to say this because I chid the Roman people, when, overheated by gratitude for the services I had done them, they desired to make me perpetual consul and dictator. Hear this, and blush. What I refused to accept, you snatched by force.

Caesar. Tiberius Gracchus reproached you with the inconsistency of your conduct, when, after refusing these offers, you so little respected the tribunitian authority. But thus it must happen. We are naturally fond of the idea of liberty till we come to suffer by it, or find it an impediment to some predominant passion; and then we wish to control it, as you did most despotically, by refusing to submit to the justice of the State.

Scipio. I have answered before to that charge. Tiberius Gracchus himself, though my personal enemy, thought it became him to stop the proceedings against me, not for my sake, but for the honour of my country, whose dignity suffered with mine. Nevertheless I acknowledge my conduct in that business was not absolutely blameless. The generous pride of virtue was too strong in my mind. It made me forget I was creating a dangerous precedent in declining to plead to a legal accusation brought against me by a magistrate invested with the majesty of the whole Roman people. It made me unjustly accuse my country of ingratitude when she had shown herself grateful, even beyond the true bounds of policy and justice, by not inflicting upon me any penalty for so irregular a proceeding. But, at the same time, what a proof did I give of moderation and respect for her liberty, when my utmost resentment could impel me to nothing more violent than a voluntary retreat and quiet banishment of myself from the city of Rome! Scipio Africanus offended, and living a private man in a country-house at Liternum, was an example of more use to secure the equality of the Roman commonwealth than all the power of its tribunes.

Caesar. I had rather have been thrown down the Tarpeian Rock than have retired, as you did, to the obscurity of a village, after acting the first part on the greatest theatre of the world.

Scipio. A usurper exalted on the highest throne of the universe is not so glorious as I was in that obscure retirement. I hear, indeed, that you, Caesar, have been deified by the flattery of some of your successors. But the impartial judgment of history has consecrated my name, and ranks me in the first class of heroes and patriots; whereas, the highest praise her records, even under the dominion usurped by your family, have given to you, is, that your courage and talents were equal to the object your ambition aspired to, the empire of the world; and that you exercised a sovereignty unjustly acquired with a magnanimous clemency. But it would have been better for your country, and better for mankind, if you had never existed.

DIALOGUE XXX. PLATO - DIOGENES.

Diogenes. Plato, stand off. A true philosopher as I was, is no company for a courtier of the tyrant of Syracuse. I would avoid you as one infected with the most noisome of plagues, the plague of slavery.

Plato. He who can mistake a brutal pride and savage indecency of manners for freedom may naturally think that the being in a court (however virtuous one's conduct, however free one's language there) is slavery. But I was taught by my great master, the incomparable Socrates, that the business of true philosophy is to consult and promote the happiness of society. She must not, therefore, be confined to a tub or a cell. Her sphere is in senates or the cabinets of kings. While your sect is employed in snarling at the great or buffooning with the vulgar, she is counselling those who govern nations, infusing into their minds humanity, justice, temperance, and the love of true glory, resisting their passions when they transport them beyond the bounds of virtue, and fortifying their reason by the antidotes she administers against the poison of flattery.

Diogenes. You mean to have me understand that you went to the court of the Younger Dionysius to give him antidotes against the poison of flattery. But I say he sent for you only to sweeten the cup, by mixing it more agreeably, and rendering the flavour more delicate. His vanity was too nice for the nauseous common draught; but your seasoning gave it a relish which made it go down most delightfully, and intoxicated him more than ever. Oh, there is no flatterer half so dangerous to a prince as a fawning philosopher!

Plato. If you call it fawning that I did not treat him with such unmannerly rudeness as you did Alexander the Great when he visited you at Athens, I have nothing to say. But, in truth, I made my company agreeable to him, not for any mean ends which regarded only myself, but that I might be useful both to him and to his people. I endeavoured to give a right turn to his vanity; and know, Diogenes, that whosoever will serve mankind, but more especially princes, must compound with their weaknesses, and take as much pains to gain them over to virtue, by an honest and prudent complaisance, as others do to seduce them from it by a criminal adulation.

Diogenes. A little of my sagacity would have shown you that if this was your purpose your labour was lost in that court. Why did not you go and preach chastity to Lais? A philosopher in a brothel, reading lectures on the beauty of continence and decency, is not a more ridiculous animal than a philosopher in the cabinet, or at the table of a tyrant, descanting on liberty and public spirit! What effect had the lessons of your famous disciple Aristotle upon Alexander the Great, a prince far more capable of receiving instruction than the Younger Dionysius? Did they hinder him from killing his best friend, Clitus, for speaking to him with freedom, or from fancying himself a god because he was adored by the wretched slaves he had vanquished? When I desired him not to stand between me and the sun, I humbled his pride more, and consequently did him more good, than Aristotle had done by all his formal precepts.

Plato. Yet he owed to those precepts that, notwithstanding his excesses, he appeared not unworthy of the empire of the world. Had the tutor of his youth gone with him into Asia and continued always at his ear, the authority of that wise and virtuous man might have been able to stop him, even in the riot of conquest, from giving way to those passions which dishonoured his character.

Diogenes. If he had gone into Asia, and had not flattered the king as obsequiously as Haephestion, he would, like Callisthenes, whom he sent thither as his deputy, have been put to death for high treason. The man who will not flatter must live independent, as I did, and prefer a tub to a palace.

Plato. Do you pretend, Diogenes, that because you were never in a court, you never flattered? How did you gain the affection of the people of Athens but by soothing their ruling passion, the desire of hearing their superiors abused? Your cynic railing was to them the most acceptable flattery. This you well understood, and made your court to the vulgar, always envious and malignant, by trying to lower all dignity and confound all order. You made your court, I say, as servilely, and with as much offence to virtue, as the basest flatterer ever did to the most corrupted prince. But true philosophy will disdain to act either of these parts. Neither in the assemblies of the people, nor in the cabinets of kings, will she obtain favour by fomenting any bad dispositions. If her endeavours to do good prove unsuccessful, she will retire with honour, as an honest physician departs from the house of a patient whose distemper he finds incurable, or who refuses to take the remedies he prescribes. But if she succeeds, if, like the music of Orpheus, her sweet persuasions can mitigate the ferocity of the multitude and tame their minds to a due obedience of laws and reverence of magistrates; or if she can form a Timoleon or a Numa Pompilius to the government of a state, how meritorious is the work! One king, nay, one minister or counsellor of state, imbued with her precepts is of more value than all the speculative, retired philosophers or cynical revilers of princes and magistrates that ever lived upon earth.

Diogenes. Don't tell me of the music of Orpheus, and of his taming wild beasts. A wild beast brought to crouch and lick the hand of a master, is a much viler animal than he was in his natural state of ferocity. You seem to think that the business of philosophy is to polish men into slaves; but I say, it is to teach them to assert, with an untamed and generous spirit, their independence and freedom. You profess to instruct those who want to ride their fellow-creatures, how to do it with an easy and gentle rein; but I would have them thrown off, and trampled under the feet of all their deluded or insulted equals, on whose backs they have mounted. Which of us two is the truest friend to mankind?

Plato. According to your notions all government is destructive to liberty; but I think that no liberty can subsist without government. A state of society is the natural state of mankind. They are impelled to it by their wants, their infirmities, their affections. The laws of society are rules of life and action necessary to secure their happiness in that state. Government is the due enforcing of those laws. That government is the best which does this post effectually, and most equally; and that people is the freest which is most submissively obedient to such a government.

Diogenes. Show me the government which makes no other use of its power than duly to enforce the laws of society, and I will own it is entitled to the most absolute submission from all its subjects.

Plato. I cannot show you perfection in human institutions. It is far more easy to blame them than it is to amend them, much may be wrong in the best: but a good man respects the laws and the magistrates of his country.

Diogenes. As for the laws of my country, I did so far respect them as not to philosophise to the prejudice of the first and greatest principle of nature and of wisdom, self-preservation. Though I loved to prate about high matters as well as Socrates, I did not choose to drink hemlock after his example. But you might as well have bid me love an ugly woman, because she was dressed up in the gown of Lais, as respect a fool or a knave, because he was attired in the robe of a magistrate.

Plato. All I desired of you was, not to amuse yourself and the populace by throwing dirt upon the robe of a magistrate, merely because he wore that robe, and you did not.

Diogenes. A philosopher cannot better display his wisdom than by throwing contempt on that pageantry which the ignorant multitude gaze at with a senseless veneration.

Plato. He who tries to make the multitude venerate nothing is more senseless than they. Wise men have endeavoured to excite an awful reverence in the minds of the vulgar for external ceremonies and forms, in order to secure their obedience to religion and government, of which these are the symbols. Can a philosopher desire to defeat that good purpose?

Diogenes. Yes, if he sees it abused to support the evil purposes of superstition and tyranny.

Plato. May not the abuse be corrected without losing the benefit? Is there no difference between reformation and destruction.

Diogenes. Half-measures do nothing. He who desires to reform must not be afraid to pull down.

Plato. I know that you and your sect are for pulling down everything that is above your own level. Pride and envy are the motives that set you all to work. Nor can one wonder that passions, the influence of which is so general, should give you many disciples and many admirers.

Diogenes. When you have established your Republic, if you will admit me into it I promise you to be there a most respectful subject.

Plato. I am conscious, Diogenes, that my Republic was imaginary, and could never be established. But they show as little knowledge of what is practicable in politics as I did in that book, who suppose that the liberty of any civil society can be maintained by the destruction of order and decency or promoted by the petulance of unbridled defamation.

Diogenes. I never knew any government angry at defamation, when it fell on those who disliked or obstructed its measures. But I well remember that the thirty tyrants at Athens called opposition to them the destruction of order and decency.

Plato. Things are not altered by names.

Diogenes. No, but names have a strange power to impose on weak understandings. If, when you were in Egypt, you had laughed at the worship of an onion, the priests would have called you an atheist, and the people would have stoned you. But I presume that, to have the honour of being initiated into the mysteries of that reverend hierarchy, you bowed as low to it as any of their devout disciples. Unfortunately my neck was not so pliant, and therefore I was never initiated into the mysteries either of religion or government, but was feared or hated by all who thought it their interest to make them be respected.

Plato. Your vanity found its account in that fear and that hatred. The high priest of a deity or the ruler of a state is much less distinguished from the vulgar herd of mankind than the scoffer at all religion and the despiser of all dominion. But let us end our dispute. I feel my folly in continuing to argue with one who in reasoning does not seek to come at truth, but merely to show his wit. Adieu, Diogenes; I am going to converse with the shades of Pythagoras, Solon, and Bias. You may jest with Aristophanes or rail with Thersites.

DIALOGUE XXXI. ARISTIDES – PHOCION - DEMOSTHENES.

Aristides. How could it happen that Athens, after having recovered an equality with Sparta, should be forced to submit to the dominion of Macedon when she had two such great men as Phocion and Demosthenes at the head of her State?

Phocion. It happened because our opinions of her interests in foreign affairs were totally different; which made us act with a constant and pernicious opposition the one to the other.

Aristides. I wish to hear from you both (if you will indulge my curiosity) on what principles you could form such contrary judgments concerning points of such moment to the safety of your country, which you equally loved.

Demosthenes. My principles were the same with yours, Aristides. I laboured to maintain the independence of Athens against the encroaching ambition of Macedon, as you had maintained it against that of Persia. I saw that our own strength was unequal to the enterprise; but what we could not do alone I thought might be done by a union of the principal states of Greece, such a union as had been formed by you and Themistocles in opposition to the Persians. To effect this was the great, the constant aim of my policy; and, though traversed in it by many whom the gold of Macedon had corrupted, and by Phocion, whom alone, of all the enemies to my system, I must acquit of corruption, I so far succeeded, that I brought into the field of Chaeronea an army equal to Philip's. The event was unfortunate; but Aristides will not judge of the merits of a statesman by the accidents of war.

Phocion. Do not imagine, Aristides, that I was less desirous than Demosthenes to preserve the independence and liberty of my country. But, before I engaged the Athenians in a war not absolutely necessary, I thought it proper to consider what the event of a battle would probably be. That which I feared came to pass: the Macedonians were victorious, and Athens was ruined.

Demosthenes. Would Athens not have been ruined if no battle had been fought? Could you, Phocion, think it safety to have our freedom depend on the moderation of Philip? And what had we else to protect us, if no confederacy had been formed to resist his ambition?

Phocion. I saw no wisdom in accelerating the downfall of my country by a rash activity in provoking the resentment of an enemy, whose arms, I foretold, would in the issue prove superior, not only to ours, but to those of any confederacy we were able to form. My maxim was, that a state which cannot make itself stronger than any of its neighbours, should live in friendship with that power which is the strongest. But the more apparent it was that our strength was inferior to that of Macedon, the more you laboured to induce us, by all the vehemence of your oratory, to take such measures as tended to render Philip our enemy, and exasperate him more against us than any other nation. This I thought a rash conduct. It was not by orations that the dangerous war you had kindled could finally be determined; nor did your triumphs over me in an assembly of the people intimidate any Macedonian in the field of Chaeronea, or stop you yourself from flying out of that field.

Demosthenes. My flight from thence, I must own, was ignominious to me; but it affects not the question we are agitating now, whether the counsels I gave to the people of Athens, as a statesman and a public minister, were right or wrong. When first I excited them to make war against Philip, the victories gained by Chabrias, in which you, Phocion, had a share (particularly that of Naxos, which completely restored to us the empire of the sea), had enabled us to maintain, not only our own liberty, but that of all Greece, in the defence of which we had formerly acquired so much glory, and which our ancestors thought so important to the safety and independence of Athens. Philip's power was but beginning, and supported itself more by craft than force. I saw, and I warned my countrymen in due time, how impolitic it would be to suffer his machinations to be carried on with success, and his strength to increase by continual acquisitions, without resistance. I exposed the weakness of that narrow, that short-sighted policy, which looked no farther than to our own immediate borders, and imagined that whatsoever lay out of those bounds was foreign to our interests, and unworthy of our care. The force of my remonstrances roused the Athenians to a more vigilant conduct. Then it was that the orators whom Philip had corrupted loudly inveighed against me, as alarming the people with imaginary dangers, and drawing them into quarrels in which they had really no concern. This language, and the fair professions of Philip, who was perfectly skilled in the royal art of dissembling, were often so prevalent, that many favourable opportunities of defeating his designs were unhappily lost. Yet sometimes, by the spirit with which I animated the Athenians and other neighbouring states, I stopped the progress of his arms, and opposed to him such obstacles as cost him much time and much labour to remove. You yourself, Phocion, at the head of fleets and armies sent against him by decrees which I had proposed, vanquished his troops in Eubaea, and saved from him Byzantium, with other cities of our allies on the coasts of the Hellespont, from which you drove him with shame.

Phocion. The proper use of those advantages was to secure a peace to Athens, which they inclined him to keep. His ambition was checked, but his forces were not so much diminished as to render it safe to provoke him to further hostilities.

Demosthenes. His courage and policy were indeed so superior to ours that, notwithstanding his defeats, he was soon in a condition to pursue the great plan of conquest and dominion which he had formed long before, and from which he never desisted. Thus, through indolence on our side and activity on his, things were brought to such a crisis that I saw no hope of delivering all Greece from his yoke, but by confederating against him the Athenians and the Thebans, which league I effected. Was it not better to fight for the independence of our country in conjunction with Thebes than alone? Would a battle lost in Boeotia be so fatal to Athens as one lost in our own territory and under our own walls?

Phocion. You may remember that when you were eagerly urging this argument I desired you to consider, not where we should fight, but how we should be conquerors; for, if we were vanquished, all sorts of evils and dangers would be instantly at our gates.

Aristides. Did not you tell me, Demosthenes, when you began to speak upon this subject, that you brought into the field of Chaeronea an army equal to Philip's?

Demosthenes. I did, and believe that Phocion will not contradict me.

Aristides. But, though equal in number, it was, perhaps, much inferior to the Macedonians in valour and military discipline.

Demosthenes. The courage shown by our army excited the admiration of Philip himself, and their discipline was inferior to none in Greece.

Aristides. What then occasioned their defeat?

Demosthenes. The bad conduct of their generals.

Aristides. Why was the command not given to Phocion, whose abilities had been proved on so many other occasions? Was it offered to him, and did he refuse to accept it? You are silent, Demosthenes. I understand your silence. You are unwilling to tell me that, having the power, by your influence over the people, to confer the command on what Athenian you pleased, you were induced, by the spirit of party, to lay aside a great general who had been always successful, who had the chief confidence of your troops and of your allies, in order to give it to men zealous indeed for your measures and full of military ardour, but of little capacity or experience in the conduct of a war. You cannot plead that, if Phocion had led your troops against Philip, there was any danger of his basely betraying his trust. Phocion could not be a traitor. You had seen him serve the Republic and conquer for it in wars, the undertaking of which he had strenuously opposed, in wars with Philip. How could you then be so negligent of the safety of your country as not to employ him in this, the most dangerous of all she ever had waged? If Chares and Lysicles, the two generals you chose to conduct it, had commanded the Grecian forces at Marathon and Plataea we should have lost those battles. All the men whom you sent to fight the Macedonians under such leaders were victims to the animosity between you and Phocion, which made you deprive them of the necessary benefit of his wise direction. This I think the worst blemish of your administration. In other parts of your conduct I not only acquit but greatly applaud and admire you. With the sagacity of a most consummate statesman you penetrated the deepest designs of Philip, you saw all the dangers which threatened Greece from that quarter while they were yet at a distance, you exhorted your countrymen to make a timely provision for their future security, you spread the alarm through all the neighbouring states, you combined the most powerful in a confederacy with Athens, you carried the war out of Attica, which (let Phocion say what he will) was safer than meeting it there, you brought it, after all that had been done by the enemy to strengthen himself and weaken us, after the loss of Amphipolis, Olynthus, and Potidaea, the outguards of Athens, you brought it, I say, to the decision of a battle with equal forces. When this could be effected there was evidently nothing so desperate in our circumstances as to justify an inaction which might probably make them worse, but could not make them better. Phocion thinks that a state which cannot itself be the strongest should live in friendship with that power which is the strongest. But in my opinion such friendship is no better than servitude. It is more advisable to endeavour to supply what is wanting in our own strength by a conjunction with others who are equally in danger. This method of preventing the ruin of our country was tried by Demosthenes. Nor yet did he neglect, by all practicable means, to augment at the same time our internal resources. I have heard that when he found the Public Treasure exhausted he replenished it, with very great peril to himself, by bringing into it money appropriated before to the entertainment of the people, against the express prohibition of a popular law, which made it death to propose the application thereof to any other use. This was virtue, this was true and genuine patriotism. He owed all his importance and power in the State to the favour of the people; yet, in order to serve the State, he did not fear, at the evident hazard of his life, to offend their darling passion and appeal against it to their reason.

Phocion. For this action I praise him. It was, indeed, far more dangerous for a minister at Athens to violate that absurd and extravagant law than any of those of Solon. But though he restored our finances, he could not restore our lost virtue; he could not give that firm health, that vigour to the State, which is the result of pure morals, of strict order and civil discipline, of integrity in the old, and obedience in the young. I therefore dreaded a conflict with the solid strength of Macedon, where corruption had yet made but a very small progress, and was happy that Demosthenes did not oblige me, against my own inclination, to be the general of such a people in such war.

Aristides. I fear that your just contempt of the greater number of those who composed the democracy so disgusted you with this mode and form of government, that you were as averse to serve under it as others with less ability and virtue than you were desirous of obtruding themselves into its service. But though such a reluctance proceeds from a very noble cause, and seems agreeable to the dignity of a great mind in bad times, yet it is a fault against the highest of moral obligations, the love of our country. For, how unworthy soever individuals may be, the public is always respectable, always dear to the virtuous.

Phocion. True; but no obligation can lie upon a citizen to seek a public charge when he foresees that his obtaining of it will be useless to his country. Would you have had me solicit the command of an army which I believed would be beaten?

Aristides. It is not permitted to a State to despair of its safety till its utmost efforts have been made without success. If you had commanded the army at Chaeronea you might possibly have changed the event of the day; but, if you had not, you would have died more honourably there than in a prison at Athens, betrayed by a vain confidence in the insecure friendship of a perfidious Macedonian.

DIALOGUE XXXII. MARCUS AURELIUS PHILOSOPHUS - SERVIUS TULLIUS.

Servius Tullius. Yes, Marcus, though I own you to have been the first of mankind in virtue and goodness, though, while you governed, Philosophy sat on the throne and diffused the benign influences of her administration over the whole Roman Empire, yet as a king I might, perhaps, pretend to a merit even superior to yours.

Marcus Aurelius. That philosophy you ascribe to me has taught me to feel my own defects, and to venerate the virtues of other men. Tell me, therefore, in what consisted the superiority of your merit as a king.

Servius Tullius. It consisted in this, that I gave my people freedom. I diminished, I limited the kingly power, when it was placed in my hands. I need not tell you that the plan of government instituted by me was adopted by the Romans when they had driven out Tarquin, the destroyer of their liberty; and gave its form to that republic, composed of a due mixture of the regal, aristocratical, and democratical powers, the strength and wisdom of which subdued the world. Thus all the glory of that great people, who for many ages excelled the rest of mankind in the arts of war and of policy, belongs originally to me.

Marcus Aurelius. There is much truth in what you say. But would not the Romans have done better if, after the expulsion of Tarquin, they had vested the regal power in a limited monarch, instead of placing it in two annual elective magistrates with the title of consuls? This was a great deviation from your plan of government, and, I think, an unwise one. For a divided royalty is a solecism, an absurdity in politics. Nor was the regal power committed to the administration of consuls continued in their hands long enough to enable them to finish any difficult war or other act of great moment. From hence arose a necessity of prolonging their commands beyond the legal term; of shortening the interval prescribed by the laws between the elections to those offices; and of granting extraordinary commissions and powers, by all which the Republic was in the end destroyed.

Servius Tullius. The revolution which ensued upon the death of Lucretia was made with so much anger that it is no wonder the Romans abolished in their fury the name of king, and desired to weaken a power the exercise of which had been so grievous, though the doing this was attended with all the inconveniences you have justly observed. But, if anger acted too violently in reforming abuses, philosophy might have wisely corrected that error. Marcus Aurelius might have new-modelled the constitution of Rome. He might have made it a limited monarchy, leaving to the emperors all the power that was necessary to govern a wide-extended empire, and to the Senate and people all the liberty that could be consistent with order and obedience to government, a liberty purged of faction and guarded against anarchy.

Marcus Aurelius. I should have been happy indeed if it had been in my power to do such good to my country. But the gods themselves cannot force their blessings on men who by their vices are become incapable to receive them. Liberty, like power, is only good for those who possess it when it is under the constant direction of virtue. No laws can have force enough to hinder it from degenerating into faction and anarchy, where the morals of a nation are depraved; and continued habits of vice will eradicate the very love of it out of the hearts of a people. A Marcus Brutus in my time could not have drawn to his standard a single legion of Romans. But, further, it is certain that the spirit of liberty is absolutely incompatible with the spirit of conquest. To keep great conquered nations in subjection and obedience, great standing armies are necessary. The generals of those armies will not long remain subjects; and whoever acquires dominion by the sword must rule by the sword. If he does not destroy liberty, liberty will destroy him.

Servius Tullius. Do you then justify Augustus for the change he made in the Roman government?

Marcus Aurelius. I do not, for Augustus had no lawful authority to make that change. His power was usurpation and breach of trust. But the government which he seized with a violent hand came to me by a lawful and established rule of succession.

Servius Tullius. Can any length of establishment make despotism lawful? Is not liberty an inherent, inalienable right of mankind?

Marcus Aurelius. They have an inherent right to be governed by laws, not by arbitrary will. But forms of government may, and must, be occasionally changed, with the consent of the people. When I reigned over them the Romans were governed by laws.

Servius Tullius. Yes, because your moderation and the precepts of that philosophy in which your youth had been tutored inclined you to make the laws the rules of your government and the bounds of your power. But if you had desired to govern otherwise, had they power to restrain you?

Marcus Aurelius. They had not. The imperial authority in my time had no limitations.

Servius Tullius. Rome therefore was in reality as much enslaved under you as under your son; and you left him the power of tyrannising over it by hereditary right?

Marcus Aurelius. I did; and the conclusion of that tyranny was his murder.

Servius Tullius. Unhappy father! unhappy king! what a detestable thing is absolute monarchy when even the virtues of Marcus Aurelius could not hinder it from being destructive to his family and pernicious to his country any longer than the period of his own life. But how happy is that kingdom in which a limited monarch presides over a state so justly poised that it guards itself from such evils, and has no need to take refuge in arbitrary power against the dangers of anarchy, which is almost as bad a resource as it would be for a ship to run itself on a rock in order to escape from the agitation of a tempest.

www.ingramcontent.com/pod-product-compliance
Lightning Source LLC
Chambersburg PA
CBHW071414170626
46811CB00003B/1392